Dotty

Dreads a Disaster

By

Diane Ezzard

Book 2 in the Dotty
Drinkwater Mystery Series

Other Books in the Series: -

Dotty Dishes the Dirt - prequel
1. Dotty Dices with Death
2. Dotty Dreads a Disaster
3. Dotty Dabbles with Danger
4. Dotty Discovers Diamonds
5. Dotty Deals with a Dilemma

Other books by Diane Ezzard

The Sophie Brown mystery series –

My Dark Decline – prequel

1. I Know Your Every Move
2. As Sick As Our Secrets
3. The Sinister Gathering
4. Resentments and Revenge
5. A Life Lost
6. The Killing Cult

Website: http://dezzardwriter.com/
Email: support@dezzardwriter.com
Facebook: https://www.facebook.com/dezzardwriter/
Twitter: https://twitter.com/diane_ezzard

Newsletter Sign-up

I hope you enjoy reading my novel as much as I enjoyed writing it. I am looking to build a relationship up with my readers, so occasionally I will be sending out newsletters. These will include otherwise untold information about the characters, things about myself, and other bits of news.

I would love you to join us and in return for giving me your email which will never be passed on to third parties, you will receive exciting offers and give-aways not found anywhere else.

You can find the sign-up page on my website at:

http://dezzardwriter.com/mc4wp-form-preview

TABLE OF CONTENTS

Other books by the author

Newsletter Sign up

Table of Contents

Novel

Newsletter sign up reminder

Reviews

About the Author /Acknowledgements

Blurbs and extracts from other books

Bibliography with links

she could relax. It had been a hard slog making enough chocolates for the two-day event. As soon as everything was packed away, she planned to treat herself to a long, relaxing soak in the bath. She deserved some pampering after her hard work.

Her new chocolate venture was proving to be physically exhausting. Any notions of building an empire the size of Cadbury's had gone out the window. Making chocolates took effort. Her bones ached from standing all day. Whilst she enjoyed the work, she hadn't anticipated how demanding it would be and how much it would affect her poor feet. Every night when she got in the bath, her weary limbs ached. It was worse than gardening! Still, at least she could eat her wares, so that was a bonus. Being chief taster, a treat was in store for her every time she came up with a new recipe flavour as she had to sample it first. Everyone had their favourites. Her dad liked the dark chocolate chilli, her mum preferred the white chocolate laced with Bailey's. Her own number one was the Tia Maria and her brother would just gobble the lot if she let him.

She hummed away as she scrubbed the work surfaces. She took off her apron and folded it up to throw in the laundry basket later. Her phone pinged. She looked down, checked the screen and smiled. Her friend, Kylie was popping along tomorrow to help with her stall. Good, that meant Dotty could wander around to see the other vendors. She liked to network and find out how everyone was doing. Most stallholders attended the same events. She knew many of them now, and she considered them like family. Hers was a fledgling business and although things were going well, she still had a lot to learn. She only set up her website last week, and that was a task and a half. Thankfully, Joe was computer savvy so had helped her.

The following morning, it felt like the crack of dawn when the alarm went off. It was 6.00 am. As much as she wanted to turn over and have a lie-in, she couldn't afford to dawdle. Dotty worked regularly at craft fairs and farmer's markets but sometimes if she turned up late, she was punished by being given the worst spot. Even as a novice at retailing, she sussed how important a prime site was. Today, she had to take what was given as places had already been allocated. Still, the Spring Fair always got a good turnout. The locals supported it and came out in their droves. Competition was fierce amongst them for prizes in the horticultural tent. There were four events a year, one for each season and the glory of winning was better than the prizes themselves. It wasn't the garden centre vouchers that everyone fought over; it was the knowledge that they had outdone others in the community, some of whom gloated for months if they received a prized rosette.

Dotty was soon up and out, motoring down the bypass to the large meadow where the event was held. Stewards on site directed the traffic to their parking spots. She'd purchased a wheeled carrier to put her boxes on and she scurried along, eager to get set up in time for the opening and the onslaught of customers. Business was slow to start but things started picking up by mid-morning. Kylie sent Dotty a text to say she was on her way. Dotty was busy cutting up samples for people to try when she heard the familiar voice of her neighbour, Betty Simpson.

"That wretched man. Someone should shoot him." Betty's arms flapped around. Even without asking, Dotty guessed who she was talking about — Nigel Hastings or nasty Nigel as he was affectionately known. His bombastic, pedantic nature got everyone's backs up. He was the main reason Dotty hadn't submitted an entry into the flower arranging category this year. She was still reeling from last year's remarks that she overworked her tulips and relied too much on her daffodils. It was outrageous. She thought he had no idea about modern arrangements and should be struck off, but she kept that comment to herself for fear of reprisals.

"What's Nigel done this time, Betty?"

"He says my rubber plant was submitted too late. It's ridiculous. I had it there in the nick of time. If the other judges, Edna Salcombe or Christine Beckley had been there, they would have allowed it, but no, he says I was two minutes late with my submission. I will be complaining to the committee, mark my words."

"He's obviously not trying to win any friends. I haven't forgiven him for his comments last year about my floral display. It took me ages to prepare and his remarks were nothing short of derogatory. If someone bumped him off with a dose of arsenic in his tea, I wouldn't lose any sleep over it."

Dotty looked up to see young Ruth Winters walking through from the horticultural tent wiping her eyes.

"What's wrong, Ruth?" Dotty might have guessed.

"It's that horrible fat old judge, nasty Nigel." Ruth sniffled.

"What's he done now?"

"He told me to go home and stick to playing with dolls rather than growing cacti. He has no idea the work

I put into tending to those plants. To be brushed aside like that hurts."

"Take no notice of him. He's probably jealous of your achievements at such a young age."

"It's not right. Someone should do something about him."

"Maybe if enough of us complain, the committee will take action." Dotty lightly stroked Ruth's forearm.

"That won't happen. He's been judging for too long. He has too much influence in the local community." Betty had been eavesdropping and threw her two-penneth in.

Kylie arrived and Dotty went back behind her stall and recounted what happened.

"I don't know why everyone gets so worked up over cabbages and carrots," Kylie commented, bemused by the fuss.

"Yes, but for some folk, it is all they care about. It gives them a sense of standing, winning a prize here."

"They should get a life." Dotty thought that sounded rich coming from Kylie whose greatest achievement in life was winning her cycling proficiency test. She soared to great heights professionally — she was a barmaid at The Old Six Bells pub. Dotty kept her mouth shut. After all, her friend had come to help her for free. She couldn't afford to upset her, not if she wanted time for a mooch around the fair later.

Kylie put on an apron and got to work straightaway. She was a good salesperson and Dotty was grateful for her support even if she bullied the customers into buying. There was a lull in visitors just after midday, so Dotty asked Kylie if she minded holding the fort while she had a walk around.

"No, be my guest. I can manage. I'll call you on your mobile if I get a busload of customers drop by."

Dotty walked through looking at the craft stalls. She was tempted to buy an art print for her bedroom wall but talked herself out of it. Sometimes at these events, she spent more than she made. She strolled into the vegetable tent expecting judging to be well under way. The two lady judges stood in a circle with some of the competitors.

"I don't know where he's got to. He should have been here ten minutes ago," Edna said, looking at her watch.

"If he doesn't hurry up, we'll have to start without him," Christine replied. Dotty sloped through to look at the floral displays. Although they were nice, she could have done a better job than most of them. Sadly, she'd been too busy this year making chocolates to consider an entry and still felt wounded by last year's comments.

Walking outside, she smelt the distinctive aroma from the barbecued hog roast as it wafted up her nostrils. She was tempted into buying a pulled pork sandwich and she strolled out towards a bench by the duck pond to eat it. She was about to sit down when she noticed something floating in the water.

Dotty shook her head and frowned. It looked like someone had dumped some clothes in. They should know better than discard jumble that way. She walked over to the edge of the tiny lake. Her eyes were still trained on the clothes gathered up.

Suddenly she gasped. That wasn't just a clump of clothes she could see, there was a body wearing them!

Chapter 2

Dotty raced back to the main tent.

"Help, help. Someone has drowned in the lake."

Montgomery Carruthers was quick off the mark and for all his ageing years, was agile enough to dive in towards the body. A crowd watched as he performed a lifesaving act that he last administered in his youth. Back then, he helped a young boy who got into difficulties while out at sea, in Torquay. This was different. It was a large grey-haired elderly man and someone he knew well. The body that looked like a beached whale was pumped but for all Montgomery's sterling efforts, there was no hope. Any sign of life had expired. Edna Salcombe crouched down in front of the body.

"Give him CPR. Keep going."

"It's no use, Edna. He's gone blue. It's too late."

"No, no, he can't be dead. Quick, do something."

Dotty thought about starting up a rendition of the Bee Gees "Staying Alive" to keep the momentum going but then wisely stopped herself from saying anything. Nigel Hastings wasn't well-liked, but it was hardly time for a singsong. Word soon got around the fair about the incident. The horror of the situation was like a Mexican wave of people's tongues. The Chinese whispers were out in force and rippled from tent to tent. Many rushed over to see what had happened. A small crowd gathered. Kylie joined in to find out what the fuss was about. She rubbed her hands together glad she hadn't missed the action.

Before long, the place was dripping in police and ambulance personnel. It was only when Nigel's body was covered with a sheet that Dotty wondered if she should have done more. If she'd dived in rather than gone for help, would he have been saved? She convinced herself, it was unlikely. She didn't want any guilt eating away at her. Secretly, she knew the real reason she hadn't gone in the water was because her hair was her pride and joy. Getting it wet wasn't an option, plus the water in the muddy duck pond looked gross.

Dotty groaned when she saw who was leading the case. Her and DS Collins had met on several occasions in the past and Dotty couldn't abide the woman. Dotty listened as the police officer gave out orders to her staff.

"Get those people away from here," she shouted. "Did anyone see Nigel enter the water?" She called to the small crowd gathered leering at the water's edge. Everyone turned their backs and talked in little huddles. Some began walking away. That was what they thought about the detective's question. She would be lucky to get any co-operation from anyone in the area. Most folk weren't fans of Nigel.

"I want a word with you, young lady. I believe you spotted the body." Dotty sighed. She didn't want to be obstructive, but DS Collins' people skills bordered on bullying tactics in her opinion. Dotty stood nodding.

"Chop, chop, then," DS Collins clapped her hands. "Get your butt over here while we run through some questions." Dotty felt the police presence was over the top. After all, there was no suspicion of foul play, at this stage at least. It was probably because Nigel was such a high-profile member of the local community. Even in death, he could metaphorically click his fingers, and everyone would jump to it, just as they did when he was alive.

Dotty did as ordered and went and sat in the police car to make a statement. Sadly, neither of her two favourite policemen, Wayne or Dave was on the scene today. She overheard DS Collins ordering some of her colleagues about.

"I want you to check his movements before he entered the water. What the blazes was he doing in the lake? Did he fall? Had he been drinking? Could someone have pushed him in? Does anyone know if he had a heart condition? Get everyone interviewed who was in the vicinity. Speak to anyone who saw him in the build-up to this. I don't like it. Something's not right. Look, forensics have arrived. Seal the area off."

Dotty listened to DS Collins bossing everyone around. That job wouldn't suit her. Dotty was no good at telling anyone what to do. The life of a police officer had never interested her, much to her dad's disappointment. Dotty watched as a police tent was erected next to the water's edge. By the look of things, the police must suspect foul play.

"Now, Dotty. How are you and how's your dad?" DS Collins jumped in the back of the police car with her. This was a turn of events. The police officer's tone changed dramatically. Dotty hadn't known her to be a friendly type on the previous meetings they had. Was it because DS Collins was after information from her or was Dotty just being cynical?

"We're both well. Dad has settled into his retirement now. He was sorry to leave the force at first, but he enjoys his golf and his gardening, anything, as long as it's not getting under mum's feet."

"He was a well-respected copper, your dad. We lost a good 'un there. Now then, Dotty. Do you want to run through how you made the discovery?"

Dotty explained how she thought the mass was some old clothes that had been thrown in, initially. She related how she ran for help rather than diving in herself because she wasn't a strong swimmer. That wasn't strictly true. If she was honest, she could only imagine entering cold murky water under protest or if a child or animal was in danger. Her auburn shoulder-length hair had been tied back but the thought of getting it wet, much least in the stagnant waters of the lake abhorred her. Plus, she would have looked a dreadful sight if her mascara ran.

Dotty's looks were important to her. She almost always wore makeup, and she loved experimenting with new colours and styles. Because she liked vintage fashion, she used colours that were popular it that era. Bright red lipstick and black eyeliner were staples in Dotty's look.

"And was anyone else around when you walked around the lake?"

"No, I didn't see anyone."

"I see." DS Collins looked at her then at the notes she had made. "What was the name of the chap who came to the rescue?"

"Montgomery Carruthers." DS Collins scribbled down the name. "Oh, this blasted pen's run out," she said, throwing the pen on the floor of the vehicle.

"Here gov, take mine," the young police officer who sat quietly in the front of the car passed her a biro. Dotty had forgotten he was there.

"Was anyone else around the area, at the time, Dotty?"

"The nearest tent to the lake is the fortune teller's. There was a small crowd stood outside, but no one there I recognised."

"Okay." DS Collins looked outside the vehicle. A member of the forensic team walked towards the car. DS Collins hutched up her body and opened the door.

As she climbed out, she called to Dotty, "That'll be all for now, thanks, Dotty."

"We'll have the samples off to the lab in a jiffy. We've taken swaps from his mouth. It looked like he'd vomited at some stage. There were food particles stuck to his clothing," the woman in the white overalls said.

Oh, yuck, Dotty thought as she listened in wondering how Nigel lost his life. Had he drowned or was he pushed?

Chapter 3

Nigel Hastings was found dead on the first day of the two-day fair. The committee held an urgent emergency meeting and decided that the show must go on. There was too much at stake financially from sponsorship deals. Cancelling was unthinkable. The last time they cancelled the show was down to destruction because of the great storm back in the eighties. The number of trees that came crashing down caused by the extratropical cyclone in 1987 was unsurpassed. Gale-force winds caused substantial damage in the area the day before the Autumn Fair was due to take place. Schools had to be closed. People couldn't go about their business. Trees were strewn everywhere on that occasion and whilst Nigel's death was a serious matter, the consensus was he would have wanted the fair to continue in his absence. Only Edna Salcombe protested. She thought the event should have been cancelled out of respect for Nigel. Everyone else disagreed. They argued that Nigel himself would have been a staunch supporter for the fair to be a success. Even Nigel's ex-wife, Judith who was at the event agreed that he would have insisted everything go ahead as normal. Dotty was secretly pleased about that. She invested a lot of time and money preparing her confectionery. Their shelf-life might have meant the chocolates lasting another week or two but not in the vast quantities she brought to the country fair. As it turned out, she did well and sold the lot.

On Sunday, Kylie turned up again to help. Dotty suspected that Kylie helped herself to a few too many of Dotty's chocolates but as she couldn't afford to pay her friend, she said nothing. Kylie saw it as a perk of the job and encouraged Dotty to walk around the fair when it was quiet in the afternoon.

Dotty chatted to a few of the other stallholders after bumping into the postman and the local vicar. She smiled and continued weaving through the circuit of stands. She had her eye on a lovely patchwork cushion. Unable to resist, she bought it to put away ready for when she eventually moved out into her own flat. She was doing what her grandma called saving for her bottom drawer. Back in her grandma's day, that was what girls did, hoarding items for when they got wed. Dotty would love to find someone to marry but hadn't met Mr Right yet. She thought about her two policeman friends, Dave and Wayne. Would she ever settle down with either of them and follow in her mum's footsteps by marrying a copper?

After yesterday's gruesome find, she decided not to venture too near the lake today. She walked outside and stopped outside the fortune teller's tent. A blackboard leaned against the entrance advertising the cost of various types of reading. Reggae music came from inside. Dotty's shoulders bounced up and down, then her feet started tapping. There was something about listening to Bob Marley that made her feel jolly and want to dance. A large West Indian lady appeared in the doorway. She swished her plaited hair and wiggled her hips with her arms flapping in time to the music.

"Yeah man, do you like my music?" She continued to dance, rolling her hands in a circular fashion.

"I love a bit of reggae. It always puts me in a good mood." Dotty smiled.

"Me too." The woman laughed so loud it made Dotty jump. The bangles on the woman's arms jangled.

Every finger displayed at least one ring. She took hold of Dotty's hand.

"Let me read your cards. I'll do it for half price."

"I… I don't know." Dotty looked across the lake and back. She couldn't think of an excuse quick enough to wriggle out of it. The woman looked at Dotty's palm and stroked her thumb across it.

"I can see you have a creative talent. I hope you are using it, my dear."

"Err, well yes." The woman's comment convinced Dotty that she should give it a bash. After all, it was only a bit of light-hearted fun.

"Come, follow me." The woman brushed past the beads that covered the entrance to the tiny room inside the tent. "Please, take a seat. My name is Delphinia."

"I'm Dotty."

"Pleased to meet you, Dotty." Both women sat down. "Please, choose a pack of cards." Dotty looked down at the table. There were four different sets. Each one looked well worn. She chose the one with the picture of a tree on the back. She thought it appeared the most hopeful. Dotty only had her fortune told once before. That was on a trip to Brighton. On that occasion, she was told she would be married and have three kids by now. That didn't come to fruition, so she would take anything she heard with a pinch of salt. Her dad moaned about fortune-tellers and clairvoyants from an early age, so it was something she generally steered clear of. Sometimes she was intrigued to know what the future held, but it had been drummed into her by her dad that she was the master of her own destiny.

So far, she hadn't been doing a very good job of that. Dotty stumbled from one relationship to another, never finding someone suitable. She had been the same with jobs. It was hard for her to make her mind up what she wanted out of life. She was curious to know what Delphinia would tell her. Dotty watched as Delphinia shuffled the pack. Dotty was mesmerised by her heavy jewellery and she had the longest fingernails that Dotty had ever seen.

"Are you a Gemini?" she asked Dotty.

"Yes," Dotty frowned. "How did you know that?"

"I sense it from your demeanour. You seem restless. It is hard to get you to settle down long enough for you to take passion or anything else seriously. Am I right? That is what you want to know about, isn't it? I can tell you are intrigued to hear about how your love life will turn out."

"Aren't we all?" Dotty laughed nervously, stunned by the accuracy of the woman.

"You haven't met him yet, so don't waste your time with anyone on the scene at the moment."

"Oh, I see." Dotty couldn't help but feel a tad disappointed by that news. The cards were laid out across the table. Delphinia pointed at the first one, the emperor.

"You have been influenced by an older person who holds fast to tradition. He has protected you in the past. He may be domineering and stubborn at times, but he only wants what is best for you. He is there to support you in your ventures." Dotty knew she meant her dad. A vision came into her head of her dad shouting at the mess she left in the kitchen. Maybe Delphinia hadn't got it quite correct on the supportive front. "Although he often displays good judgement, he doesn't always get things right." This woman is good, Dotty thought. Delphinia stopped concentrating on the cards for a moment and touched her temple. "I'm getting the letter R. Do you know anyone with that initial?"

"I have a friend called Rachel." Dotty raised her eyebrows.

"No, this is a male." Dotty groaned.

"I had an ex-partner called Ray. He was a pain and took ages to get rid of." Delphina stared at Dotty. "I... I don't mean literally get rid of. I didn't bump him off or anything. Could it be him?" She gave a nervous laugh.

"Possibly. I must warn you to be careful around this person." Delphinia looked down and turned the next card. "Oh dear, Dotty. Things aren't going your way right now, are they? The ten of swords isn't good news. You need to manage a despairing situation in the best way you can. You are likely to have an unwelcome surprise soon. There's some sort of failure here," she said tapping the card. "Something untoward is coming. Let's see if we can find better news." Delphinia smiled and turned over the next card. Dotty sighed. It didn't look good. It was the death card. "Don't worry, this card can signify new beginnings after the death of something. Although..." Delphinia's eyes narrowed. There was something about the way she gazed at Dotty which made her believe she could see into her soul.

"It was me who found the body yesterday. Could that be what you see?"

"What, you found that dreadful man?" Delphinia shuddered and closed her eyes. She clasped her hands together and spoke in what Dotty could only describe as gobbledegook.

"I'm praying in tongues, Lord have mercy," she said, opening one eye. "God forgive me for thinking bad thoughts about him, but I can't say I'm not happy that he is no longer with us."

"You didn't like Nigel then?"

"No, I did not. Do you know, he called me a charlatan and tried to get me banned from the fair? It was outrageous. He was not a very nice man, not nice at all." She tutted. "Sorry, where were we? Ah yes, death. It seems to surround you, my dear, I'm afraid."

Dotty was glad when the ordeal was over. Although she was amazed at some of Delphinia's revelations, she didn't like the idea of bad news coming her way. She was about to leave the tent when she was almost bowled over by a young black man.

"Winston, what have I told you about getting under my feet when I am working? What do you want now?"

"I want some money for a burger." He scowled at Dotty.

"Here." Delphinia reached into her purse, her arms jangling. She passed him a twenty-pound note. "Make sure you bring me the change." Then she turned to Dotty and said, "Sorry about that. My son is always hungry. I wish he'd stayed at home. He's like a human dustbin."

Dotty left Delphinia and walked back to her chocolate stall. Something disturbed her about meeting the woman and she couldn't put her finger on what.

Chapter 4

Dotty's dad put down the newspaper. He folded it up and placed it neatly inside the magazine rack. Dotty watched him. She was having a ten-minute breather from making her chocolates. He'd tidied his paper away so precisely, yet it would be out again in a short while when he opened it do to the crossword. Dotty couldn't understand the importance of neatness. Pete's motto was — tidy place, tidy mind. Maybe he was onto something there because Dotty's mind could get smutty. Spending so much time with Kylie caused it, either that or her barren love life.

She thought about the two men she had designs on. They weren't exactly in her life yet. She snogged Wayne on New Year's Eve and danced with Dave, but nothing progressed any further. Neither of them used social media. Dotty wondered if it was a police security instruction so that criminals that they locked up wouldn't know their whereabouts and be able to revenge target them. She had Wayne's number, but she wouldn't contact him. If he wanted to take her out as he suggested, then he could do the running. Dotty was old-fashioned like that and believed in courtship.

"You like to go foraging, don't you, Dotty?"

"Yes, why, Dad?"

"I've been talking to my old pal from forensics, Ian Frampton. He tells me it was a dodgy dose of mushrooms that killed old Nigel Hastings. He didn't drown. It was a severe reaction to mushrooms."

"Mushrooms? What, was he poisoned?"

"Well, that's the six-million-dollar question that the police will have to find out. How did those mushrooms get inside his system?"

"I often pick mushrooms up at Dosier Wood when I'm out walking with Winnie." At the sound of her name, the little poodle padded into the conservatory where Dotty and her dad sat talking. She wagged her tail. Dotty bent down and stroked her.

"Yes, we were talking about you, weren't we?" Dotty smiled at Winnie. She spoke in the same tone as she would if speaking to a tiny baby. Winnie put her front paws up onto the sofa.

"No, down, Winnie. There's a good dog." Dotty's tone became more adult-like. Pete watched his daughter with the family pet. He knew how much she idolised that dog.

"Funnily enough, I read an article about mushrooms in *Gardener's Weekly*. Let me find it." Pete rummaged through the magazines and pulled one out. "Here it is." He flicked through the pages and opened it out to a centrefold showing mushrooms of differing shapes and sizes. He pointed to one of the pictures.

"You'd be hard-pressed for thinking that one wasn't edible. Look at this, the *Amanita phalloides* or death cap looks like a common garden mushroom. There are whole hosts of deadly poisonous mushrooms that could make you very poorly or kill you."

"Oh, how awful. I wonder what he had for his lunch. Could it have been something he ate that killed him?"

"Quite possibly, and if that was the case, then how did it get in his stomach?"

It wasn't long before that question was answered. Dotty received a call, the following week, from Millie. Dotty had struck up a friendship recently with Millie after she booked the next table at the local farmer's market. Millie was another foodie like Dotty and both girls liked to discuss recipes and cookery shows. Millie ran a homemade soup stall at weekends. Dotty's phone rang, and she saw it was Millie's number.

"Millie, are you there?" All Dotty could hear was crying. Finally, Millie spoke amid the sobs.

"They think I killed him."

"What are you talking about, Millie?" The poor girl was beside herself.

"Nigel Hastings was killed after eating soup he bought from my stall. I served up three different soups that day — mushroom, a beef broth and a pea and ham soup. Nigel had the first portion of the mushroom soup."

"Well, if it was the mushrooms in the soup that killed Nigel, how come no one else was affected?"

"Because the person who bought the next cup brought his back with a fly in it. When I opened the lid, there was also a large beetle that somehow got into the pot, so I threw the rest of the batch away. Luckily, only Nigel had some, otherwise, I might have killed a whole bunch of others." Millie's wailing was so loud that Dotty had to hold the phone away from her ear.

"This sounds very suspicious."

"That's why the police had me down at the station all day. They've only just released me. What am I going to do? They've told me not to leave the country."

"Why? Were you planning on running away?"

"No, but they think I'm guilty or they wouldn't have said that."

"I'm sure they say that to everyone."

"Did they say it to you? I mean you found the body."

"No, but it might have been an oversight on their part. They probably meant to tell me. They only say it because they may need to ask you more questions. I wouldn't worry. If they believed you were guilty, they wouldn't have released you." Millie's wails grew louder.

But Millie was worried to the point that when she phoned Dotty again the following day, she told her she was feeling suicidal over the trauma of the incident.

"You mustn't get yourself upset like this. I will be here for you and do all I can to help. Please call me if you need me." Dotty realised then she must do what she could to support her friend. This called for immediate action. She phoned her two best friends, Kylie and Rachel and they arranged to meet up at the Strawberry tea rooms, their regular meeting place.

"Have you brought your pad, Rachel?" Dotty asked her friend whose middle name should be efficiency. Rachel worked in an office as an admin assistant and loved bringing her corporate knowledge to try out on her friends. They had regular brainstorming sessions, much to Dotty and Kylie's annoyance. This time Dotty took charge. "I'm worried about Millie. This business with Nigel Hastings is having a massive impact on her health. We've got to help her."

"You don't think she killed him then?" Kylie took a bite out of her cheese and ham toastie. The way she tore at it, she looked like a cave woman who hadn't eaten for a week. The other two glared at her.

"Of course, she didn't kill him. That poor woman hasn't got an unkind bone in her body."

"I just wanted to put it out there and check. I mean, if we were the police, we would suspect everyone, even you, Dotty."

"Dotty's nostrils flared. Kylie had the knack of saying throwaway comments that were so unkind sometimes.

"Well, if that's the case, then you could also have done it. You were in the area."

"Ah, but I wasn't as close as you were to the action. I didn't find a body."

"Will you two stop it. This is getting ridiculous. We know that you or Millie didn't kill anyone." Rachel took on the role of peacemaker like a member of the United Nations. "Now let's see who we have as suspects. Have you got your pen ready, Dotty? Write this down," she said, wagging her finger towards the lined pad. "Who didn't like nasty Nigel?"

"It would be easier to do a list of who liked him." Dotty frowned.

"Oh dear, well, let's change our tack here. Who had a motive, and who had the opportunity to kill him?"

"From what I hear, he recently got divorced. His ex-wife may be a prime suspect. It's usually someone known to the victim that carried out the crime." Kylie smiled.

"You're sounding more and more like Miss Marple every day, Kylie," Rachel said.

"What about your auntie Flo, Kylie? She was upset when he disqualified her cauliflower and asparagus." Dotty raised her eyebrows and looked across at her friend.

"Oh, come on, you don't mean to tell me Auntie Flo would bump someone off over vegetables."

"She was angry when I saw her in the competitor's tent. They virtually had to restrain her when Nigel walked through."

"Still, it's a bit far-fetched."

"True, but as you said yourself, when we're brainstorming, we shouldn't discount anyone. Isn't that right, Rachel?" Dotty winked at Rachel who flashed a big beaming grin across her face and nodded.

"I don't think we've got much more at this stage. Dotty. If you speak to Millie and find out who was in the vicinity at her soup stand. Somehow, someone sneaked poisonous mushrooms into her soup and talked Nigel into having some. Kylie, if you check out your auntie Flo. I'll tackle the other two judges and we'll find out more about what nasty Nigel got up to when he was alive. Someone must know something."

"It's a scary thought," said Kylie, "but we have a murderer in our village."

Chapter 5

Dotty met up with Millie the following day. She wanted to chat with her about the fair while everything was still fresh in her mind. It was a windy spring day, yet mild enough to meet in the park. Dotty wrapped up well, zipping up her dark green Barbour jacket. She popped on a matching green beanie hat and took Winnie along. It meant Winnie got a walk out and Dotty felt good having her poodle there. She hadn't realised Millie also owned a dog, and she had brought along Schmeichel, her Great Dane. The two women, canines in tow, approached the rendezvous site. Millie wore a cream woollen coat with a blue and black scarf around her neck. Her flat knee-high black boots made her look sophisticated.

Dotty guessed that things wouldn't go to plan. Her trusty dog had been her companion long enough, so she knew when something wasn't right. She watched as the hairs of Winnie's coat stood on end. Then her tail started rotating, not the usual friendly wag, more like a helicopter blade going round and round. Winnie looked about to pounce. The two dogs barked. If Millie and Dotty wanted the meeting to be private, then the disturbing sounds coming from their dogs put paid to that. Millie tugged on the lead.

"Schmeichel, come here. There's a good dog." Size-wise, Winnie was no match for Schmeichel. It wasn't since she was a puppy that Winnie had attacked another dog, but today she did her best to harass the bigger animal.

"Winnie, behave yourself." Dotty had never seen her poodle get so agitated before. Eventually, both animals calmed down, but when everything seemed relaxed, and the two women weren't looking, Winnie nipped at Schmeichel's leg.

"Winnie, you naughty dog. I'm so sorry, Millie. I don't know what's got into her today." Millie didn't look too pleased but was too nice to say anything. After both dogs were restrained and tied to fencing far enough apart to avert an altercation, the women could finally discuss the tragedy.

"What shall I do, Dotty? This murder will affect my business. No one will buy anything off me now if they think I might poison them. It's a good job it's not my only income but I rely on the extra I get from the soup stall."

"If it weren't so serious, it would be laughable. I mean, the idea that you would try to kill people in that way is unthinkable. My friends and I will help all we can. I don't like to see anyone going through something as awful as this. I can't imagine what it must be like."

At this, Millie started to cry. The two dogs looked on, both with cocked heads. Dotty passed Millie a tissue.

"I know it's painful for you to talk about but in order to help, I need you to remember everyone who came to your stall before Nigel was served."

"What, you think someone put something in my soup to frame me?"

"Well no, I hadn't considered that, but it is a possibility. Is there anyone who doesn't like you?"

"Only my ex, Royston but he's too stupid and incompetent to be devious."

"Who else was in the vicinity at the time?"

"The police asked me this. I remember Flo Whiteside coming over. She wanted to try a sample but then bought nothing. Some people are like that, you know, they just want all the freebies they can get. They don't realise the hard work that goes on behind the scenes trying to make a living."

"Tell me about it. I have the same problem. Was anyone else around?"

"Christine Beckley, one of the other judges came over asking to see my insurance certificate. I was annoyed about that. I'd sent everything to them online, and they said they couldn't find it. Then after that, let me get this right." Millie looked up to her right. "Yes," she nodded. "I asked Judith Hastings to mind my stall while I nipped to the loo."

"Judith, as in Nigel's ex-wife?"

"That's right."

"That's very interesting."

"Did you serve mushroom soup to anyone else?"

"Only Delphinia's son. I can never remember his name."

"Winston," Dotty prompted.

"Yes, yes, of course, Winston. He had some soup but brought it back pretty sharpish."

"Why, what was wrong with it?"

"He said there was a fly in it." Millie put her hand on her heart. "You know, God must have been looking after me that day. If he hadn't brought his soup back, I may have killed half of Billingshurst but after that incident, I threw the batch away. Ironically, I didn't want Nigel to get wind of it and close me down for not complying with health and safety. He was a stickler for his rules and regulations."

"Don't I just know it. It's a shame there's no CCTV in the area. Can you think of anyone else who may have witnessed anything, especially around the time when you went to spend a penny?"

"No, they were the only people I remember seeing close by. I wouldn't like to think of any of them being capable of killing Nigel."

"But someone did, and they had to have the opportunity to carry the dastardly deed out. From what you said, by disappearing for five or ten minutes, you could have given a carte blanche golden chance to someone on a plate." The two women looked at each other and nodded.

Millie's skin had gone ashen, anaemic-looking. This whole incident had taken its toll. Her striking green eyes were almost devoid of colour, like a leaf with its last gasp of chlorophyll. Even though her black hair was tied back, the contrast of its colour against her pale skin made her appear more ghostly. By the puffiness under her eyes, Dotty imagined the poor woman wasn't getting much sleep. She had been through the wringer.

Dotty didn't believe for one minute that Millie was involved. It didn't take an expert to realise that after looking at her appearance. She wondered whether she ought to say as much to either of her two policemen friends, Wayne or Dave. Somehow, she didn't think they'd be too happy with her interference. She couldn't call on her dad either. Now, he had retired from the force, he was more interested in playing golf than fighting crime. No, if Dotty helped Millie, she would have to solve this one herself with support from her friends. From what Millie told her, the number one suspect now had to be Judith Hastings.

"Thanks for the chat, Dotty."

"No, thank you. If you think of anything else that will help, get in touch. Plus, any more suicidal thoughts ring me, even if it's the middle of the night. Do you promise?"

"I promise."

As they parted to go their separate ways, Dotty went to hug Millie. At that moment, Winnie started barking. Dotty turned to see what the noise was about. Schmeichel spotted a rabbit and chased after it with Millie taking tight hold of his rein. Schmeichel's speed was too much for Millie though and she caught her foot on a branch and toppled over. Not wanting to let go of her dog, she was pulled along the ground. Unfortunately, after the recent bout of rain, the terrain was soft and moist. Dotty gasped wide-eyed at the sight of Millie being dragged through the mud.

Dotty's hand went over her mouth. For once she was speechless as Millie came to a halt and got up out of a slimy puddle. Her cream coat was ruined. She looked like she had a mudpack on her face. Dotty wanted to laugh but knew how insensitive that would be.

"Schmeichel, how could you?" Millie threw his lead to the ground in disgust. "Look at the mess! Poor Millie really was having a bad old time of things.

Chapter 6

Tracking down Judith Hastings wasn't as easy as Dotty expected. Eventually, she got her address from the electoral roll. Her house was within walking distance from Dotty's home, so she had a stroll down the lane with Winnie in tow.

Judith Hastings stood in the front garden of her property. She wore wellington boots and gardening gloves and had a trowel in her hand. There were no signs of her doing anything with it. Dotty stood on the pavement watching her over the Hastings' fence. She took in the smell of freshly mown grass.

"Get that wretched beast away from me," Judith shouted so loud, all the neighbourhood could hear.

"Come here, Winnie. There's a good girl." Dotty patted her dog and turned to the woman she had been searching out for the past week. "She won't bite, she's well trained." Dotty secretly crossed her fingers. "I wanted to pass on my condolences, Mrs Hastings."

"Don't give me that. You probably hated Nigel as much as the rest of those wolves who were after his blood."

"No, I didn't know him that well."

"So, what are you doing here then? Have you come to have a good old gloat at my misery?" Dotty frowned.

"No, of course not. I'm sure this must be a difficult time for you. You can't have had it easy when you were with him. By all accounts, he was a difficult man to be around."

Judith and Nigel had lived in one of the larger pre-war semis since their fifth wedding anniversary. That was a long time ago now and although Judith had wanted to modernise the home and put an extension on, it hadn't happened. Her mind was already ticking away with how best to spend Nigel's money when probate came through.

The ink was only just dry on her divorce papers and the bottom line was, she wasn't happy with the settlement she received. On the other hand, Nigel had been forced out of the marital home by the decree absolute. He reluctantly moved in with Mrs Kelsall, one of their neighbours, as a lodger, three weeks previously. A "for sale" sign hung in the Hastings' garden but Judith hoped that could be taken down now. She had no intention of selling the property she lived in for half her life. All this information, Dotty gleaned from her nosey neighbour, Betty Simpson. She was now hopeful that meeting Judith Hastings in the flesh, she would find out more.

"No one has any idea what I went through with that man." Judith looked up to the sky which threatened rain. She shook her head.

"I genuinely am sorry for your loss. I can't imagine how difficult things must be for you right now. If there is anything I can do to help, just know that the offer is there."

Judith's face softened. She thought for a moment, then turned to Dotty.

"Well, there is something. I've got that many people coming over at the moment. I've got the police taking up my time, then there's the vicar to talk to about the funeral service, whenever that may be. The estate agent has to come back because I'm taking the property off the market. There's no way I could contemplate selling up now this tragedy has happened. It would be far too stressful for me and lead me into an early grave. My doctor said as much when I saw him last. I've had lots of friends and family passing on their condolences. This place feels like Grand Central station right now, with the comings and goings. Anyway, what I wanted to ask was, would you be a darling and get me a few groceries? I am chained to the house today because of the visitors I'm expecting including the TV man."

What Judith failed to mention was that the TV man wasn't coming to carry out any repairs, he was bringing a brand new, state-of-the-art TV. Judith had promised herself one with her settlement money, ever since filing for divorce.

"I don't mind. Anything I can do to help. As I said, you must be going through a tough time and I want you to know that I am thinking of you."

"That's very kind of you, dear. If you pop through and wait in the hall while I get my list ready. Don't bring your dog in though. I'm allergic to dog hairs."

Dotty tied Winnie up to the post in the porch and walked into the house. She followed Judith into the large kitchen. There was pine everywhere from the French dresser to the cupboards, chairs and tables. Even the shelving was pine.

"I know what you're thinking, how outdated it is."

"Not at all, I was admiring the view out of your window." Dotty was good at telling little white lies. It came naturally to her. Judith looked out the back window at the vast garden and nodded.

"Nigel was a typical accountant. He was so tight-fisted. We never had the kitchen updated in all the years we've been here. The only reason he let me have a new washing machine was because the old one broke. I've dreamt of a new luxury kitchen for years, so now I'll get my wish." She smiled and looked around the room. Both sets of eyes circled around then came to a stop on the kitchen table. There, spread out was an array of paperwork. Judith noticed Dotty's frown. "I must apologise about the mess. I went yesterday and picked up Nigel's mail from Mrs Kelsall's. That's why the paperwork is out. I've been sifting through it all. After about an hour of looking at that lot," she said wafting her hand towards the pile of letters, "I'd had enough and decided the garden needed me more and the bank statements could wait. It was never my forte. The thing was Nigel was a member of every club going. He didn't believe that any of them could run properly without his involvement so there's a lot to get through."

Dotty heard that Nigel was on lots of committees. She glanced at the letters sprawled out on the table. There was one from the Horticultural Society, another from the Billingshurst Beekeeper's Club and the third one she spotted wasn't an organisation she had heard of before – the White Brethren Society. The reason she noticed that one was because the paper was of a cheaper quality than the others, plus the note had been handwritten. The details were obscured from view. She didn't envy Judith having to sort that lot out. It never dawned on her up until that point, how much was involved with someone's passing. The life they left behind didn't just stop. It had to be sorted and finalised.

Dotty wondered if there were any clues in amongst that paperwork to give any indication why Nigel was killed. Whilst she would have offered to help with the paperwork, she thought it may sound too obvious and look like she was prying. She would have to tread carefully. There were plenty of questions she wanted to ask Judith but for now, she would settle for shopping for groceries for her. She would bide her time. After all, this woman could be a potential killer.

Chapter 7

Kylie arranged to see her auntie Flo. They were quite close, and Kylie normally called at least once a month. She felt guilty of late because she'd been so busy, she hadn't seen her in a while.

"Yes, do come over, dear. It's ages since we had a good old chin wag. It's about time we put the world to rights. I can tell you about my new little business venture." Flo laughed. Kylie didn't think from her friendly tone that she sounded like a murderer, but she knew she must keep an open mind.

The way Flo dressed you would never guess she was in her late sixties. Her cropped brown-tinted hair was gelled to give it height. She wore smart jeans with a tear at the knee. Her light brown bomber-style leather jacket set off her tanned face which was courtesy of a tube of St Tropez. Her brown jumper and matching neck scarf completed the ensemble. Kylie admitted her style made her look far younger than Uncle Chris. He also wore jeans, but his were falling off and showed off his builder's crack at the back – not a pretty sight. He nodded at Kylie then continued reading his paper. The two women went through into the conservatory. Kylie couldn't help but get a whiff of a stench coming from the house that didn't smell legal.

"So, you've set up a new business. That's exciting, Auntie Flo."

"Yes, it is rather." Flo smiled and clapped her hands together. Kylie waited to hear more.

"Are you going to tell me about it?" They sat on the cream-coloured sofa facing each other.

"Well, it started with my arthritis."

"Your arthritis?" Kylie frowned.

"That's right, dear. I was in an awful lot of pain. I can't tell you how bad it gets. It's debilitating. Sometimes I haven't been able to move out of the house for days."

"Oh, that's awful. I never realised it got so bad."

"Not anymore."

"No."

"I found the solution."

"Tell me more."

"A mate of Chris's down the pub suggested I try cannabis, so I smoked a joint and bingo, it did the trick."

"Right," Kylie's mouth gaped open. Not wanting to look too surprised by this revelation she gulped and tried to continue a normal conversation. "I heard there is something in cannabis to help reduce pain, that's why they recommend cannabis oil."

"That stuff is a load of cobblers. It didn't work for me, but the real McCoy did."

"So, what's this got to do with your new business?"

"I grow my own now and sell it." Kylie spluttered and blinked.

"What, you're a drug dealer?"

"It's not like that. I just have a few regular customers I supply. They're elderly friends in the same boat as me. We're not taking it to get high, but that is a nice bonus sometimes." Flo nudged Kylie.

"But you could end up in prison. You know it's illegal, don't you?"

"Don't worry about me. I'm too small fry for the police to worry about."

"How did you start up this enterprise?"

"I sent Chris to Amsterdam to buy some. We kept it hush-hush from the family. I don't suppose your dad would approve. You know what a killjoy he can be. Then I researched on the net how to grow my own. I don't smoke it in the house." Flo said that as though it would be a crime to do such a thing.

"Is there no other way you can take it? I wouldn't like to see you getting into trouble over this and it is quite pungent," Kylie said, holding her nose.

"There's not a lot I can do about the smell other than sticking air fresheners all over the house. I've tried other lotions and potions for the pain, and I wouldn't want to become addicted to painkillers. There's no other remedy like this one."

"But the smell is gross, and it's such an obvious pong."

"Oh dear, is it that bad? I suppose we've got used to it. Chris doesn't seem to mind. He's probably high from the aroma half the time."

"I don't know what to say, Auntie Flo. I'm flabbergasted. You must be careful though."

"It's okay, the local drug dealers know me. I told them I'm not trying to encroach on their patch. We had a good chat and we understand each other." She winked. "I'm only interested in supplying people in pain. I do have some morals, you know."

"Mm."

"Anyway, enough about me. How's your love life, young lady? Have you found someone to shack up with yet?" Kylie smiled at her auntie's quest to learn language more appropriate for someone younger than her years. Auntie Flo had never been one to conform. She didn't have her first tattoo until her late forties and now had more ink than Kylie. Flo was the epitome of growing old disgracefully.

"No, I'm still looking. I've not been as lucky as you." Whilst Kylie had been shocked at her auntie's revelations, she thought Flo would be even more so if she knew Kylie was seeing a married man.

"Well, I'm glad you've popped over. We don't see enough of you. Let me make you an Irish coffee as a treat. I've also got some cake I'd like you to try. It's a new recipe of mine."

"It's a bit early for any booze for me. Can I have a cup of tea?"

"Certainly, if that's what you want but you must try my cake." Flo had a cheeky glint in her eye.

Kylie joined Flo in the kitchen while they chatted some more. Flo still liked to do some things the old-fashioned way and used tea leaves in her fine white porcelain teapot that had the rose design on the side. She made her and Chris a coffee with a good dose of whisky. Kylie watched as the cream flowed over the spoon and settled at the top of the mugs. They returned to the conservatory, Flo carrying the tray. Flo held onto the lid of the teapot as she poured out the tea then cut a piece of cake off for Kylie.

"Here, get this down you. I know you're partial to a bit of fruitcake." Kylie took the small plate from Flo and immediately took a bite out of the cake.

"Mm, this is good, Auntie Flo. You must give me the recipe."

"I will, dear."

"That was a terrible do about Nigel Hastings, wasn't it?"

"Yes, the whole village is talking about it. God forgive me for saying this but it's not true that only the good die young. That man didn't get the nickname nasty for nothing. He upset so many people."

"There are plenty glad that he's dead. Does that include you, Auntie Flo?"

"Well, I wouldn't wish what happened to him on anyone. It's put me off trying those magic mushrooms that are all the rage with the young ones."

"Auntie Flo! They're hallucinogenic. They send you loopy." As Kylie said that, the room began to feel distant. "Oh, what a lovely painting of a flower that is. I'd never noticed it before." Kylie stroked the mug she drank from.

"Thank you, dear. Here, have some more tea and cake."

"Don't mind if I do. Did you see Nigel before he died?"

"I was angry with him after he disqualified my vegetables, especially my asparagus. That was my pride and joy. The last time I saw him was just before he went over to Millie's soup stand. I gave him one of my looks. You know the ones I mean, the look where I can knock a man stone dead." The significance of that sentence didn't dawn on Flo.

"Do you remember seeing anyone around the soup stall who acted suspiciously?"

"No, not really." Kylie took another bite of the delicious cake.

"Was anyone else about at the time?"

"I can't remember now. I get very forgetful, you know."

The room began to disappear in and out of focus. She couldn't remember what she'd asked. The cushion material looked so shiny. She stroked it. Everywhere became hazy. Kylie couldn't understand it. She felt spaced out, a million miles away.

"Auntie Flo, what was in that cake?"

"Marijuana, my dear."

So, that was it. Kylie was stoned.

Chapter 8

Rachel was the last of the three girls to go on her mission to find out information. She trotted along to the library where Christine Beckley worked. Christine only did part-time hours nowadays. It was enough on top of looking after her elderly parents. Ten years previously she had done a very brave thing and bought her own place. She didn't think her mother would have ever forgiven her but with her ailing years and need for support, she had to accept her daughter's offer of help. Christine had never married and as an only child had been spoilt. However, she lived under the shadow of her domineering mother for years. It was because of her mother that she never found "the one". No one was good enough for Agnes Beckley's daughter.

The nearest Christine got to marriage was when she courted Wally Sawyer. Of course, her mother didn't approve. That was only natural. He was a roofer, a job far too lowly for the prestigious librarian, according to Agnes. Wally finally agreed with Agnes on the day of his wedding and took off with Christine's best friend, Rita, an hour before the service was due to take place. Christine hadn't heard from either of them since and nor did she want to. The shame of being stood up at the altar affected her badly. She became bitter and lonely. That experience took her thirty years to get over and it was only her fondness for Nigel Hastings that finally helped her to move on. People close to her wondered what she saw in him. Maybe it was the similarity of his personality to that of her mother. They were both bossy and constantly found fault with Christine. But the fact that Nigel even noticed her was enough for Christine to see she didn't have to be the wallflower anymore. The only problem was that years with no form of close relationship meant she was emotionally immature. This was as much as Dotty and her friends knew about the lady who had been a judge at the local fairs for the longest time. Sometimes, Dotty wondered what she'd do without Betty Simpson's snippets of information. Now Rachel was tasked with finding out more.

As luck would have it, the library where Christine worked was only around the corner from Rachel's office. Rachel had never been much of a reader. At junior school, she loved everything by Enid Blyton. When she was told at high school that she had to throw away her *Famous Five* books as they were only for kids, she was mortified. She took the hump and never read another book. When there was a buzz around *Fifty Shades of Grey*, she tried to pick up reading again but it was too heavy going for her. She had lost the power of concentration.

So now here she was, sneaking up and down the aisles of books, browsing through the large print section. She'd purposely worn her long blonde hair up to make her look more like a bookworm. If she had to lend a book, just to get to speak to Christine, then so be it. She may even attempt to read one. Rachel soon spotted Christine when she walked up to the counter. Her shiny red and gold name badge was emblazoned on her chest.

Christine tinted her hair herself. That much was certain. The colour was varying shades of brown. Rachel chuckled to herself. If she had left it grey, she would have been able to promote the novel of the same name. She wore an old-fashioned thin pink cardigan over the top of an equally thin black jumper. Her skirt was a multi-coloured floral number with an elasticated waist popularised by women of a certain age who liked to shop via catalogues. The brown brogues on her feet were a typical part of the uniform for a librarian. It made Rachel think. She didn't want to morph into a typical office worker wearing black pants and a purple tailored blouse. She would have to make more effort to look different from the crowd in future. Perhaps she should take a leaf out of Dotty or Kylie's books. Dotty wasn't one to go with the crowd. She had a quirky style of her own and loved the dress style of the forties and fifties. Older members of the community commented on her looking like Rita Hayworth. Kylie, on the other hand, wore clothes with attitude. She dressed like she was going to a rock concert. In truth, she had never been to one in her life. Her goal was to get to Glastonbury one of these years, but the longer she left it, the less likely it would happen. Still, Kylie was the rock chick in the group with her endless supply of dark T-shirts promoting different groups and a hair colour that alternated between pink, blue and purple depending on her mood. Rachel's look was feminine and practical, and her favourite colour was pink. It was surprising that the three girls got on so well, they were so different, but they had been inseparable since junior school.

Rachel waited her turn behind a chap wearing glasses the size of milk bottles. She noticed he hadn't picked up one of the large print books. Maybe he was masochistic. That thought took Rachel back to the *Fifty Shades* book. She looked at him and shook her head. Linking him with bondage was a repulsive idea. Rachel sidled along and found herself in front of Christine with her shiny badge.

"I'd like to borrow this book, please, Christine." Rachel knew from her training at work that holding eye contact and calling someone by their first name was the best way to win friends and influence people. She had recently been on a rapport building course, so was pleased to put into practice the skills she picked up. For the life of her, she didn't know why she had been sent. She got on with people okay and the only people she encountered were her immediate team and of course, Harry from accounts, her new boyfriend. It wasn't as though she had a customer-facing role so needed to learn these things. But now she was glad of those new skills as she stood in front of the librarian.

"Good morning, I'd like to take this book out, please," Rachel repeated. She had picked up a copy of *Wuthering Heights* knowing it was a classic. If she was taking up reading again, then there was no better place to start than with a good old romance. Christine didn't look up. Rachel sighed. She wouldn't give up or change her tone. She repeated the sentence. There was still no response from Christine. Rachel tried one more time, a little louder.

"Ssh, ssh, ssh," came a chorus of sound from those in the vicinity. It sounded like a train going past. Christine finally looked up.

"Yes, can I help?" Rachel closed her eyes and counted to five – ten would have taken too long and there were four people behind her now in the queue.

"I'd like to borrow this book please."

"Do you have your membership card?"

"Erm no, I'm not a member."

"Then you must fill this form out first and bring it back with two forms of ID." Rachel hadn't expected so much red tape just to take a poxy book out of the library.

"Erm…" Rachel turned and glanced at the people waiting behind her.

She looked around then moved closer to Christine and whispered, "I don't know how to fill it in."

Christine passed her a pen.

"If you've got your ID with you, you can complete it now."

"Would you be able to help me with it? I'm not very good at filling forms out." Christine sighed. She could well do without the extra hassle from Rachel but these days her bosses came down hard on anyone not showing extra support to people with disabilities. Only last week the library set up an initiative to help people with dyslexia. In Rachel's case, there was nothing wrong with her ability to fill out the form, she just couldn't come up with any other way to engage Christine's attention and get close to her.

Christine huffed. "Can you take over here, Penny? I'm just going to assist this customer with her form." She indicated for Rachel to move over to the corner.

"Don't I know you?" Rachel asked Christine.

"Name." Christine pointed to where Rachel needed to write her name on the form.

"Weren't you one of the judges at the Spring Fair?" Christine's cheeks turned bright red.

"I have been a judge there for fifteen years."

"Terrible business with Nigel Hastings, wasn't it?"

"You knew him, did you?" Christine eyed Rachel with suspicion as her eyes narrowed.

"I knew more of his reputation than anything."

"And what had you heard about him?" Rachel thought the conversation had gone skew whiff. She was the one supposed to be asking the questions.

"I heard he was a tough judge and that he upset a few people."

"He had his favourites, but he was a good man and misunderstood by many."

"Is that allowed if you're a judge? I thought you had to be impartial."

"True." Christine's expression changed. She coughed. Rachel could see anger burning in her eyes.

"So, who were his favourites?"

"I'm not at liberty to say." Christine's lips narrowed.

"Oh, go on. I won't tell anyone plus he's dead now so what harm can it do."

"Let's just say there were some people who got preferential treatment from him. Address."

"Sorry?" Rachel frowned.

"Put your address in there." Christine tapped the paper. From the way Christine's demeanour changed talking about Nigel, it was obvious Rachel wouldn't get much more insight into her relationship with the man today. The pair remained silent other than Christine asking questions relevant to the form.

Rachel had gleaned little from Christine. By the time she came away from the library, she felt there was more to Christine than meets the eye. If she had the time and inclination, she may also now read up on Heathcliff's antics in *Wuthering Heights*.

Chapter 9

The three friends met up at the Strawberry tea rooms as usual at the weekend to compare notes.

"I don't think my auntie Flo had anything to do with it." Rachel poured the tea from the ceramic floral teapot.

"But without hard evidence to the contrary, we can't discount her."

"That's the sort of thing your dad might have said, him being an ex-policeman."

"Well, it's true."

"We don't seem much further forward with our enquiries. I've got an idea," Kylie said.

"O-oh." The two other girls glanced at each other. Dotty raised her eyebrows.

"Why don't we invite Delphinia to do us a reading and see if she can see anything?"

"You don't believe in that mumbo-jumbo, do you, Kylie?" Dotty pulled a face.

"If it's good enough for the police to get clairvoyants in, it's good enough for us. I mean it's not as though we have any other bright ideas on how to move forward."

"She's got a point, Dotty, and it can't do any harm. We could ask Millie to come along. It might help give Delphina extra vibes or whatever else it is she gets."

"I haven't spoken to Judith Hastings yet about what happened when she looked after Millie's stall for a period."

"Yes, but if she's the killer, she's hardly going to say she popped her batch of poisonous mushrooms in while the coast was clear." Kylie shook her head.

"No, but she may have seen someone else there."

"You can still check that out. Come on, Dotty. This will be a bit of fun."

Finally, Dotty agreed, and Kylie arranged for Delphinia to come over the following Wednesday evening to give all three girls and Millie a reading.

Kylie went to town on the arrangements. She bought some scented candles and incense. She even put on a little buffet courtesy of Sainsbury's. There were sausage rolls, pork pies, mini quiches and Prosecco chilling in the fridge.

"Gosh, you shouldn't have gone to this much trouble, Kylie," Rachel said when she arrived, the last of the group to turn up at Kylie's tiny flat. Kylie had moved out of her family home four months ago after a nasty bust-up with her mum. They still weren't on full speaking terms which meant Kylie only spoke to her if she was after something. Kylie felt her mum interfered too much in her love life. She'd have a field day if she knew Kylie was dating a married man. Maybe, seeing Kenny would end in disaster, but she would have to make her own mistakes, and no one could tell her any differently. Once Kylie wanted something, nothing would stop her getting it and she wanted Kenny from the first time she set eyes on him. She had only been in her new place a week when the toilet blocked. It wasn't the most romantic of encounters when Kenny came over to get rid of the turds lurking down the pan.

Kylie felt indebted to him. Since the blockage, her morning ablutions had been affected, due to the pungent smell from the drains. She was so repulsed by her own excrement lingering in the bathroom that her body had reacted, and she had been constipated for days. After Kenny performed his magic, Kylie let rip and couldn't hold back on that waste waiting in her bowels. She was so thankful when she came out of the toilet, she offered up her body to Kenny as a bonus for his work and he accepted. He had been coming to check Kylie's plumbing ever since.

"So long as you don't tell people you're coming over to service an old boiler, I don't mind." She smiled.

"Don't worry, I'd rather grease your nipples than the ones I normally have to work with."

Kylie loved the plumbing terms, and the innuendos tickled her. From flushed grollings to jigged olive-spantles, she now knew about ballcocks and frotting pencils.

"I'll be sucking the clenching pin tight to the arc thrust." Kenny smiled.

"I don't have a clue what that means, but it sounds sexy. Come here, lover boy." When Kylie pulled Kenny over the threshold of her front door, they went at it like rabbits, christening every room in the house. The trouble with Kylie, she was an open book. She had no qualms about discussing the finer details of her love life. Until recently, her mum had been getting an education in the Kama Sutra, which had probably pushed the mother-daughter relationship to its limit. Kylie was advised by her friends that some of her sexual exploits should be kept private to save any embarrassment, or at least be for their ears only.

Tonight, Kylie had worn a black dress with a slit up the side in the moody goth-punk style she so loved. Her black lips and thick black eyeliner added to her style. The only thing out of place was the pink fluffy slippers she wore that matched her newly tinted hair colour.

Delphinia arrived. As she got out of her dark-blue BMW, she said a little prayer to her spirit god, Jonathan for getting her there in one piece. Winston's driving was atrocious. It was too fast and erratic. He didn't take heed of his stopping distances learnt when he passed his theory test four years ago then promptly forgot everything. That was how it seemed to Delphinia. Still, she mustn't moan too much. The last time she did that, he wouldn't pick her up. Winston had a wilful side, and he was too old now to change. He took after his wayward dad. Bongo, as his dad was affectionately known, walked out of the family home while Winston was an impressionable teenager. Now he paraded around their neighbourhood on the council estate where they lived in Crawley with his many girlfriends. Bongo had plenty of money, mainly obtained by ill-gotten means. His family never saw a penny of it though. According to the powers that be, he was on benefits and out of work. Surely, even they should be able to see that something didn't add up. He swanned around in a brand-new Mercedes, much to Winston's annoyance.

His dad wasn't the only reason Winston was moody. It was as though he had been born with a negativity gene and nothing was ever right in Winston's world. He found fault with everything and everybody. Delphinia learnt over time what pushed her son's buttons. Today there had been a tension in the air as they drove along. She grabbed hold of the seat when he swung around a corner too rapidly for her liking, but Winston was upset by her reactions. He threw a load of expletives her way and told her she overreacted. Often, that was the case with Delphinia, but not on this occasion. This time, she breathed a sigh of relief when she got out of the car.

"Do you want me to give you a bell when it's time to pick me up?"

Winston didn't reply. Delphinia nodded. She understood his moods. At times like this, she wished she'd learnt to drive.

"Pick me up at ten, then." She smiled at her son who scowled back at her.

Chapter 10

"I'll go first," Kylie said. She didn't want Delphinia's strength sapping after speaking to the other side or whatever she did to foresee the future. The West Indian woman set up her stall in Kylie's bedroom. It was done out in pink and black, Kylie's two favourite colours. Even the teddy bear on the bed in between two cerise satin cushions was pink. Delphinia sat on a white rocking chair that normally stayed in the corner with half of Kylie's wardrobe hanging off it. Kylie perched on the pink fluffy dressing table stool next to her. The walls were covered with black and white photos of different bands most of whom were too obscure for anyone to have heard of.

Delphinia brought along some incense for effect and she lit it while Kylie sat watching, anticipating what she may be told. Delphinia's hair, although braided had been tied into a knot that resembled a snake curled up. The burgundy draw-string blouse she wore set off her gold jewellery. Her full skirt came down to mid-calf and was a mustard, orange and burgundy mix with an African style design. Her jewellery jangled, from the gold chains around her neck to the bangles on her hand. She also wore some unusual looking rings. One had the head of a bear; another was in the design of a skull. Her makeup was loud and heavy. Bright eyeshadow and lipstick helped to enhance her protruding eyes and lips, not that they needed any more enhancement.

She passed a crystal to Kylie and asked her to hold it and think of what she wanted answers to. There was only one question Kylie needed to know, and that was how her love life would turn out. She wasn't foolish enough to believe there could be any future with Kenny. He had a wife and children and Kylie didn't want to be labelled a home wrecker, but she was curious to find out how long they would be together.

She held the crystal, squeezing it in her palm. She closed her eyes and when she opened them Delphinia seemed to be in a trance. The older woman mumbled something. It made Kylie feel nervous, and she wondered if she was okay. Suddenly, Delphinia took the crystal stone back, placed it on the dressing table and took hold of both of Kylie's hands in hers. She nodded. Kylie hoped she couldn't read her mind because she was having smutty thoughts about Kenny and some of the things they got up to in that bedroom.

"You love your freedom, don't you, darling?" Kylie nodded. "You belong to everyone and yet to no one. No man will tie you down for a long time yet." Kylie raised her eyebrows. She had a picture of being tied down literally by Kenny. "You're not looking for a man with money."

"Am I not?" Kylie shook her head, bringing herself back into the room.

"No, you are more impressed with achievements." Kylie was more impressed with a man's bedroom prowess which she thought could include achievements.

"I suppose you are right."

"You like to flit around from one relationship to another, don't you dearie?"

"Yes, you could say that." Kylie laughed.

"Don't take this the wrong way but… I'm not sure how to put this." She glanced over at Kylie. "I would say you have an unusual code of ethics. You don't like to conform." Kylie laughed a dirty laugh. It didn't take much detective work to figure that out from Kylie's short-cropped platinum hair with the long shock of pink hair at the front. "You have many friends. Are you an Aquarius?"

"Yes, can you tell?" Kylie's eyes opened wide.

"I thought so." Delphinia looked pleased with herself. "You stay friends with your exes, don't you?"

"That's true." Kylie pictured what happened a week last Saturday. She had sex with Barry, her previous boyfriend, on the snooker table where he worked

"You're a social butterfly, adaptable and witty." Kylie enjoyed listening to the compliments. Delphinia's eyes narrowed. She put one finger under her mouth and held her chin with her thumb. "Watch that you're not taken in by someone. You can be naive."

"I don't know about that." Kylie frowned. She didn't like being deceived by anyone.

"You take what people say at face value. Just be careful. You may get into a situation that is too hot to handle."

"I think I know what you mean." Kylie didn't want to give any clues to Delphinia. If this woman knew she was seeing a married man, she may judge her. Delphinia took hold of Kylie's hand again and began to stroke the palm with her thumb. For a moment, she thought Delphinia was making a pass at her but then she pointed to the edge of her hand.

"It doesn't look like you'll have any children." Kylie wasn't worried about that. It was enough looking after herself. She didn't have a maternal bone in her body, at least not right now. She was too busy having fun. "I see that you enjoy experimenting with different ways of doing things." Kylie wasn't sure where Delphinia was going with this. All she could think about was her copy of the Kama Sutra that she'd rucked out of sight in the drawer before Delphinia arrived. "Your friends are important to you." This comment jolted Kylie back into the present. She thought about what she and her friends had previously discussed which was to get Delphinia talking about the murder to see if she came up with anything. "Is there anything you want to ask me?" the West Indian woman said.

"Have you ever been asked to help in a murder investigation?"

"Not in this country. I did when I was back home in Antigua. I once helped find the body of a little boy, thanks to a vision I had. The police had their suspicions about his disappearance but couldn't do anything without a body. I had flashes of the boy in a quarry and that was where they searched. Sadly, they found him dead but by finding his body they could arrest his killer."

"Have you had any such occurrences around Nigel Hastings." Delphinia's face changed. The sparkle from her eyes disintegrated in a moment.

"Just the mention of that man's name leaves a nasty taste in my mouth. This may be a wicked thing to say, Lord have mercy on my soul, but this world is a better place without him in it." Her words came out as a snarl. Kylie watched Delphinia shudder with disgust.

"You didn't like him then?"

"Like him?" Kylie stared as the rage built up in Delphinia's face. "I wouldn't even spit on his grave."

"He did a lot for the community. He was involved with many organisations."

"That man was a bigot and a bully. He only involved himself because he was controlling and meddlesome and wanted to rule the roost. He upset many people including me."

"Do you want to talk about it?"

"Not here, not now. It wouldn't be fair on you ladies who are paying good money for my services. Maybe, I will tell you just how evil nasty Nigel was, some other time."

"I would be all ears."

They finished their session and Kylie went to get the next person in. By the end of the night, the girls seemed suitably impressed with Delphinia, mainly because she had stroked their egos and praised them with compliments. She told Rachel she was a deep, mysterious beauty, magnetic, proud and confident and that her outward persona of being a fragile fluffy kitten was pretence. That was a brave move by Delphinia, but she hit the nail on the head when she said she became controlling once she got her man.

"You're the type of woman who looks equally good in anything from a baseball cap to a ball gown, darling. You're perceptive and you retaliate. I think you're very good at evening the score. If someone tells you a lie, you will tell them two." Rachel laughed at this comment. "You can hate with venom yet love with abandon. You're clever because you let your man think he is the boss, but he's not, is he, darling?" She winked at Rachel. "You're very much in charge." Unwittingly, she gave out her boyfriend's name and then was astounded when Delphinia mentioned him. "You're jealous of other women around Harry, aren't you, darling?" Rachel nodded wondering how this woman knew so much about her. "Did he criticise your cooking recently, and you vowed never to cook for him again?"

"Yes, that's amazing."

"Make him one of your specialities, darling. You've got a good one there. Continue keeping your home sparkling clean the way you do. It's a credit to you."

Rachel did like to keep her place neat and tidy and was blown away by Delphinia's comments.

Dotty was the least receptive of the girls. When Dotty asked her questions about her own home life, Delphinia didn't seem keen to part any knowledge.

"I'm here to talk about you, darling and can I tell you, there is a mystic aura around you. I didn't notice it last time we met but I believe you have a special gift."

Dotty raised her eyebrows. She wanted to keep an open mind around what Delphinia had to say but she wasn't convinced by her. To Dotty, this was a bit of a laugh. "If you tune into your spiritual side more, you will see beyond your simple existence and be able to interpret the movements of the universe."

"Is that what happened for you?"

"Not really, I received the gift as a child. My dreams came true. It frightened me at first, but I soon realised I was special and different." Dotty wished her dreams would come true and she would meet a man who would love her. She didn't want to focus on the strengths of her astral-spiritual connections, as Delphina suggested.

"I've been anxious since I found Nigel's body at the Spring Fair. Because of that, I feel compelled to do all I can to find his killer."

"I see your soul is troubled and I may be able to help with that. I wouldn't get involved in looking for the killer if I were you. It will only make you more stressed." She smiled. "If you want to book in for a private session, we could do some work around channelling your spiritual energies and getting more of a metaphysical balance." Dotty didn't have a clue what Delphinia was talking about, and she thought the woman was just out to make a fast buck.

"I'll think about it."

At the end of the evening, Delphinia packed her things away when her son came to pick her up. Everyone heard the car outside making a racket, sounding its horn. Delphinia got flustered.

"Oh, I can't be late for Winston. He'll have a right paddy." The horn blasted repeatedly outside. "That'll be him now." Her hands jerked and her movements shook as she pulled her shawl around her shoulders. "I better go, he gets cross if I leave him waiting." The way the horn continued to blast Winston was not a patient man. "Oh, isn't he annoying?" Kylie raised her eyebrows and nodded. They thanked Delphinia who couldn't wait to get out of the house.

Chapter 11

The four girls stayed behind to compare notes on their readings. Dotty was the least impressed of the group. She still had suspicions that Delphinia may be a charlatan, as Nigel suggested. There were a few sentiments that rung true. She hit on the fact that Dotty was a fantasist. Dotty had to agree she loved daydreaming. It took her away from the pressures of life. She also mentioned that Dotty got bored with routine. Often, her chores wouldn't get done because she was too busy planning her next great escapade. None of them ever came to fruition but then climbing Mount Everest and white water rafting down the Zambezi were rather extreme goals. In reality, she was unlikely to get further than a day out in Brighton. Thinking of which, she had a big fair in Brighton this weekend selling her chocolates. Thankfully, Kylie had offered to help again. It was so much easier when two of them attended. Putting the gazebo up on her own was a struggle. There were usually one or two able-bodied men to come to her assistance, but Dotty liked to do things for herself. Kylie was just the opposite. If there was a man about, Kylie turned into a helpless kitten.

"Delphinia doesn't think I'll end up with Kenny," Kylie said, munching on a sausage roll that was left.

"You can't be surprised about that." Rachel shook her head. "Do you think she researches us before she gets here?"

"Don't be so cynical, Rachel. Can't you just trust her powers." Kylie swigged the bottom of her glass of Prosecco.

"She asked me if I had an auntie Flo."

"What did you say?" Kylie's interest perked up.

"I told her you had one."

"It's probably because we are so close that she thought it was your auntie." Kylie put an arm around her friend. "Did she say anything about her?"

"She hinted that she may be in some sort of trouble." The girls looked at each other with eyes open wide. That was the nearest they got to Delphinia providing any useful information in finding out who killed nasty Nigel.

Although Kylie didn't suspect her auntie Flo, she couldn't get away from the fact that she had both the opportunity to pop poisonous mushrooms in the broth and the motive. There was a long-running saga between Nigel and Flo. This wasn't the first year that he had disqualified her entry. They had history between them going back years. It started when a cake Flo made for the fair collapsed. She blamed the judges for prodding her cake unnecessarily and causing it to demolish. It was supposed to be a replica of Arundel Castle and Flo had been very proud of her accomplishment. She demanded compensation and when none was forthcoming, she went to the papers about it. A photographer from the *Observer* had been at the fair at the time, so had snapped the caved-in castle. The newspaper printed a picture of Flo with the headline "Arundel Castle demolished." That edition sold four times as many copies as usual as everyone thought it was the real-life castle that had been destroyed. The judges and Nigel, in particular, were inundated with cruel comments. The trolls punished them on social media with their cutting remarks and Flo became a local hero, if only for a day. Since that incident, she believed the judges tried their utmost to find fault with any of her entries to the point where it felt like a personal vendetta against her. So, when her cauliflower and asparagus were disqualified this year, it could have been the last straw for Flo.

"Whoever murdered Nigel knew their mushrooms. They knew what they were doing. Most people wouldn't have a clue which were the poisonous varieties." Kylie was still eating leftovers.

"I suppose whoever did it could have found the information online," Dotty said.

"True, and in which case we will probably never know, but there is also the possibility that someone took a book out of the library to study the varieties. It is worth checking to see if the library stock any books relating to mushrooms and if they can provide us with information about the lenders." Kylie helped herself to a handful of crisps that were left in a dish on the table.

"Good thinking, Kylie. It's worth a try." Dotty's expression was serious.

"I'll get onto it tomorrow."

The following day, Kylie was off work so able to go along to the library. Graham, the manager at the pub where she worked had only just stopped phoning her asking her to do extra shifts. He had called her almost every day for the past three weeks. They had been short-staffed and one of the other barmaids was off sick with a broken arm. Thankfully, Graham had now recruited a temporary replacement which meant Kylie could have her life back. The extra money came in handy and she had already spent most of it. The good news about not working today meant that Kenny was coming over to see her tonight. She walked into the library with a spring in her step.

"Excuse me," she said to the librarian with wispy hair tied up in a bun. The woman looked up over her thick-rimmed glasses. "Do you have any books on mushrooms?"

"If you have a look in the gardening section, some of the books on plants have a section on fungi. We have a couple of books that specifically deal with mushrooms and toadstools. Normally, I could look the details up for you straightaway, but our main server is down." She flapped her hands in the air. "If you give me a moment, I'll show you how to search for them using our back-up method." A few minutes later, Kylie stood over her shoulder at the indexing drawers. "Thank goodness we still keep the old-fashioned card system updated." Her nimble fingers worked through the tray of cards. "Here we are, yes I was right. There are two books specifically relating to mushrooms." The librarian smiled. She seemed pleased with herself and showed Kylie which shelf to find them on. "They should both be there somewhere if they're not out on loan."

Kylie went over to look but couldn't locate either book. She called on the librarian again for her assistance.

"You've been ever so helpful. I can't thank you enough." The librarian was one of those people who loved helping others. The satisfaction she got from the praise she received was immense. A lifelong spinster, she had dedicated her life to the library. There were rumours that it was due to close. Thankfully, she was nearing retirement, so it wouldn't affect her, but she still thought it would be a sad day if that happened. The two women stood with their eyes peeled on the array of books. She checked the nature shelves.

"Oh dear, I can only think both books must be out on loan and unfortunately, I can't tell you right now because of the temporary blip with our technology."

"Would you be able to let me know when they come in or better still, tell me who loaned them?"

"Oh, I couldn't say who has them if they're out on loan."

"The thing is, Jean," Kylie said, reading the woman's name badge and moving in closer towards her. "I am a private investigator. I am investigating a murder inquiry for a client of mine." Her voice was hushed. "It may help the case immensely if I found out who had been researching mushrooms recently."

"Oh, you mean because of the death of Nigel Hastings?"

"Ssh." Kylie put her pointer finger over her lips and nodded. "This has to be between you and me."

"I see. Well, of course, I will help you all I can," Jean whispered. She looked pleased with herself for guessing who the investigation was about. "Do you have a card and I'll contact you with the information you require as soon as the computer system is up and running again?"

Kylie feigned looking for a business card. She patted down her pockets and searched in her handbag.

"Drat. It looks like I have given them all out. Here, I'll write my number on a piece of paper." She passed the scribbled note to Jean who looked as proud as a peacock as she thrust out her chest. This may be hush-hush, but she would tell her elderly parents who she lived with that she was helping in a murder inquiry. Nothing as exciting as this had ever happened to Jean before. The nearest she got to any excitement was the day the fire brigade turned up at her house. Her large-framed mother had got herself wedged in the toilet seat and couldn't get out.

"I will do all I can to help."

"Thank you, Jean." Kylie winked at the librarian and left.

Chapter 12

Kylie was running late. She needed to get back home, showered and changed before Kenny arrived. She thought about offering him something to eat but she was such a bad cook, it might put him off her. Kenny wouldn't mind. It wasn't her food he came over for. Kylie was the takeaway queen normally. She lived off fried chicken, burgers and kebabs and had the hips to prove it.

As soon as she arrived home, she rushed into the shower. Her toes flinched as she walked across the cold ceramic bathroom floor. Her mind was giddy, anticipating the night ahead. She couldn't get the picture of Kenny in the buff out of her brain. As she turned the dial on the old appliance, thousands of lukewarm droplets were released over her head. She closed her eyes as the water trickled down her back. Her thoughts still had images of Kenny and she smiled.

After she finished, she dried herself off then slumped on her bed looking up at the ceiling. She hoped this would be a night to remember. Their first encounter had been one of nerves and fumbles. Now they had shared more intimate moments, they were both more relaxed with each other. Kenny told her how much he liked to grab hold of her ample frame as he whispered his sexual fantasies in her ear. She hoped to enjoy his body for as long as she could before he got fed up of her and went back to his wife.

Kylie set the room up with some Barry White music and scented candles. The lights were dimmed as she waited for Kenny's arrival. He was early which she saw as a good sign of his eagerness. He didn't disappoint. Kenny's biceps and pecs flexed when he walked through the door. He wasted no time taking his T-shirt off. Kylie's eyes ogled his body. She was mesmerised by his torso. He wasn't waiting for any formalities such as a cup of coffee. This man meant business and had only one thing on his mind. Kylie stared shamelessly. He had ink across his chest and down his arms. The tattoos spilt over onto his back. Kylie couldn't wait to explore his body.

They kissed and Kylie led him to the bedroom. Their lovemaking was fast and furious. It was over too soon for Kylie's liking, but he had satisfied her. They lay together in bed and he told her about his day at work. Their behaviour turned to being more like that of an old married couple.

"I went over to an elderly man's place today. He had a blocked toilet. It wasn't the prettiest of jobs. When I looked in the pipes, I found out what the problem was."

"Fat turds?" Kylie asked.

"No, false teeth."

"What?"

"Yeah, he dropped his dentures down the loo without realising and he'd been wondering where they got to." Kenny laughed.

"Oh, that's gross. I wouldn't want to wear them again after knowing where they'd been." Kenny looked at the time.

"I have to shoot."

"What? Already? That's a shame. I was hoping for seconds."

"You're a nympho." He kissed the top of her forehead. If he'd kissed her any lower, he may have been tempted to stay for more.

Kylie's love life was a far cry from Dotty's. Whereas Kylie saw all the action, Dotty had seen none. There was little point having two men chasing after her if all they did was chase her by text. It wasn't in her makeup to ask a guy out but if neither Wayne nor Dave got their finger out soon, she would have to resort to stronger tactics or search elsewhere. She was sick of spending time at home watching TV every night. Even her mum and dad had more nights out than she did. She wondered if men weren't attracted to her because she still lived with at home. There would be no hanky-panky under her parents' roof. She liked to take things slowly anyway. It had taken time to get over her previous relationship. The scoundrel had never told her he was married, and it had wounded her.

Whether it was the law of attraction or some special skill Delphinia passed on to her, something spooky happened that night. She was thinking of Wayne when a message pinged through from him.

Fancy a trip to the movies and a Chinese next Thursday?

It felt eerie how she had willed him to contact her. Maybe Delphinia had super-powers after all. She made arrangements with Wayne and still had a big grin on her face when her phone rang. It was Kylie. She no doubt wanted to go into the finer details of what she and Kenny got up to.

"I've got some news," Kylie said. Dotty was surprised. Her voice wasn't as upbeat as she expected.

"Go on." Dotty waited to hear about Kylie's escapades.

"Auntie Flo has disappeared."

Chapter 13

The girls met up at the Strawberry tea rooms the following day. The anguish showed on Kylie's face. She rocked back and forth in her chair.

"I can't believe Auntie Flo would do something stupid like this. She must have lost her phone because it's not like her to be silent. There's been no news. I'm getting concerned now. It's been three days since she disappeared."

"I hate to ask you this, Kylie, but does she know anything about mushrooms?"

"Oh no, you don't think she was involved with what happened at the Spring Fair." Kylie's lips narrowed and she placed her palms down on the table.

"Her disappearance looks suspicious, you've got to admit, Kylie." Dotty's words did nothing to allay Kylie's worries. Kylie's head dropped.

"There is a glimmer of hope." Kylie glanced between the other two.

"Oh?" Rachel asked.

"She went down the pub the evening she disappeared, so she may have gone on somewhere and continued drinking. She once got so drunk after a party she went missing for five days. Maybe she's done something like that again." Kylie raised her eyebrows.

"Did anyone see where she went?"

"Uncle Chris doesn't seem too concerned. He thinks she'll surface soon. He said he'll give it a week and if she hasn't come home by then, he'll start looking."

"I'm glad I'm not married to him. I hope nothing sinister has happened to her." Rachel shuddered. "Keep us posted, Kylie. How are things with you, Dotty? Are you looking forward to your date with Wayne?"

"I suppose so."

"Only suppose?" Rachel asked. Dotty shrugged her shoulders.

"I like him but it's early days. I don't know him well enough yet and I don't want to rush into anything after what happened with the last fiasco. No more married men, thank you very much." She put her hand up like she was stopping traffic.

"There's nothing wrong with a married man if you want to spice up your life." Kylie's face brightened up, thinking of her time with Kenny. "You're still interested in Dave, aren't you? That's why you're not getting all gooey-eyed over Wayne."

"I do like Dave as well. Dave's more of a gentleman but he's very slow on the uptake. He probably doesn't fancy me."

"Oh yes he does," piped up the other two in unison. They all laughed.

"We must come up with some way to nudge him along." Kylie smiled.

"I don't want you two getting involved."

The girls chatted some more about their respective love lives. Kylie kept glancing over at the brownies on display but for the first time in ages, she resisted temptation.

"You're not even tempted by those gorgeous cream cakes. What's going on?" asked Rachel, who never ate cake.

"It's only because my stomach is off. Worrying about Auntie Flo is affecting me physically."

Dotty nodded. It wouldn't do Kylie any harm to lose a bit of weight. She might encourage her to come along to the Slimming World class that Dotty had joined.

Kylie's phone rang.

"I'll take this, girls." The noise in the café was loud with the constant chatter of the mums who regularly attended the establishment. There was also a table of elderly women celebrating one of their group's birthday. Kylie couldn't hear anything, so she took her phone outside to speak.

A few minutes later, she skipped back in with a smile on her face.

"Who was that? Kenny?" Rachel asked.

"No, better than that." Kylie's grin went from ear to ear.

"Better than Kenny? This has to be good. Come on, spill the beans." Rachel watched her sit back down. Kylie had this knack of leaving her friends in suspense when she had something important to say. It reminded Dotty of how they operated at judges houses on *X Factor*. They would keep the contestants guessing, right to the very last second, eking out the waiting game for extra suspense.

"Who was it, Kylie?" Dotty asked in a loud voice. She was losing patience with her friend.

"That was the librarian, Penny." Kylie's eyes sparkled.

"And?" Rachel drummed her fingers on the table.

"She had some news for me."

"We guessed that as she phoned you. Come on, Kylie what is it?" Rachel's fingers flapped towards Kylie, beckoning her to provide more information.

"She told me who previously lent the books on mushrooms."

"Anyone we know?" Dotty cocked her head to one side.

"Have a guess."

"Oh Kylie, stop being an idiot and tell us." Rachel slammed her hand down on the table. The women sat at the next table turned around. Kylie moved her head in closer towards her friends who did likewise.

"Christine Beckley," she mouthed.

"Wow, really?" Rachel's eyes widened, and she sat back in her seat then looked across at Dotty whose eyebrows were raised. She nodded, thinking. "I don't understand. Christine works at the library, doesn't she?"

"Yes, but I presume she still has to borrow books like the rest of us, especially if she wants to study what they contain." Kylie raised her eyebrows.

"One of us ought to pay Christine another visit. I'm happy to go," Dotty said.

Back at home, Dotty tried to figure out how to get hold of Christine's address. She checked through all the paperwork she had about the local fairs. Sometimes, they gave out addresses of those in charge but when she went through everything, there was nothing listed for Christine. Dotty decided to call in to see her good friend, Patsy at the local florist's shop. She knew Christine was a churchgoer and Patsy was married to the local vicar. Hopefully, she could find out where she lived.

The shop door pinged as Dotty walked in. She had brought Winnie along for the walk and left her outside. She didn't want her dog knocking over any vases or displays.

"Hi, Dotty. Good to see you. What brings you out on a blustery day like today?" Patsy asked. It was heading towards May, but the March winds were still out in force and it looked like rain was on the horizon. Dotty breathed in the mixed floral aromas that she loved.

"I'm after a favour, actually. I've some questions I want to ask Christine Beckley. She attends your church, I think, so I wondered if you could get her address for me."

"I'm sorry, Dotty. As much as I'd like to help, I wouldn't be able to give out personal information. I can't afford to fall foul of the data protection laws."

"I guessed that." Dotty's face looked glum. Her head bowed, looking down at the concrete floor. Patsy had been friends with Dotty since they did a flower arranging course together.

"Can't you call in the library to see her?"

"It's rather a delicate matter. I want to speak to her in private." Patsy busied herself moving buckets of mixed flowers.

"I could give her your number and ask her to contact you." Suddenly, the door pinged open. Dotty looked up. She couldn't believe her luck. In walked Christine, her hair looking more dishevelled than usual.

"Is that your dog out there?" Christine addressed Dotty, frowning.

"Yes, em, I've only popped in for a minute to see Patsy."

"it's doing a lot of barking." Dotty knew that. She could hear Winnie's impatient woofing.

"I'm going to her now." Dotty walked towards the door. The other two women watched her.

"Oh, Christine?" Dotty called over. Patsy turned away and busied herself at the counter.

"What?" Christine's tone was curt.

"I've been doing some foraging. I wondered if you could help and tell me what I can and can't eat. From what I hear, you're the expert on mushrooms."

Christine's cheeks reddened.

"I'm no expert." She cleared her throat.

"I'm curious to know more. I'm trying to eat more of the healthy, back-to-the-earth kind of foods." Christine studied her. Patsy kept her head down.

"In that case, why don't you come along to the evening class I'm running at the garden centre over the next six weeks. It's on plant food and I think you'll find it useful."

"That sounds a great idea. I'll go down and sign up. Thank you, Christine, and see you soon, Patsy." Patsy waved her friend off, wondering what she was up to.

Chapter 14

Dotty loved going to the cinema. Ever since she was a child when she used to go to the Saturday matinee, she got excited at the sight of the big screen. She hugged a huge family-sized popcorn watching the adverts. The war film wouldn't have been her first choice. She was more into romcoms, but she gladly settled for anything just to have a night out. Plus, Brad Pitt had a starring role, so it wasn't all bad. She glanced across at Wayne as he took a slurp from the small-sized coke that was actually ginormous. Goodness only knew how big the large size must be. He'd have spent the night emptying his bladder and missing half the film if he'd chosen that. His hand dived into the bucket of popcorn and he smiled at Dotty as they watched the trailers together.

She was glad he had brought her to the better of the two cinemas in the area — the one with the plush seats. It was almost like being at home, as she slouched with her feet up. She sat back to relax as the movie started and she sank into the dark red velvet chair. As the lion roared, the chatter stopped. It wasn't long before Dotty's mind hurtled back to the Second World War, the setting for the film. She imagined herself as a heroine working for the Resistance in France and helping all the Jewish children to escape. Bombs hurtled down in unison with the noises on screen. Her thoughts took a dark twist as she was sentenced to death by the Germans. Thankfully Brad's face popped up in time to save her and she re-joined the film's storyline.

Halfway through the story, one of Brad's character's mates was found dead and Dotty took a tissue out of her bag to wipe her eye. Wayne must have noticed, as he put his arm around her shoulder and kissed her cheek. She snuggled up closer to him, nuzzling against his shoulder. His blond hair flopped forward as he went in to kiss her. He still had hold of his drink, so juggling it and kissing at the same time was a daft idea. The way he petted her face, with his coke in one hand, it was obvious that disaster was about to strike. The trouble was it was hard to manoeuvre his large beaker with Dotty's hair now in his face. Unfortunately, the inevitable happened and the drink spilt onto her hair. She cringed. She wouldn't make a scene, but she was annoyed that he had taken the top off the plastic container. His excuse was that he didn't like drinking through a straw. It wasn't manly enough for him.

The accident wouldn't have happened if he'd been more careful. It wasn't as though anyone else could see him drinking through a straw, anyway. Dotty huffed. Wayne apologised, but the damage had been done. She leaned her body the other way as she squeezed out the sticky liquid from her hair strands. He obviously had no idea how important Dotty's hair was to her or how painstaking she'd been about getting the style right before she left home that evening. Every strand had been coiffured into place. It would look a ruined mess now and be all sticky and clumped together. She would have to wash it in the morning, a chore she hated. She counted to ten to stop herself from getting cross. Wayne was oblivious to any issues and Dotty's anguish. He was enjoying the film too much. It was just his cup of tea — lots of blood, guts and action. There was even a sex scene to whet his appetite. As far as he was concerned, the date was going swimmingly.

Dotty felt miserable. She was glad the lights were dimmed because her hair must look like rats' tails now. There was no way she could go for anything to eat afterwards. The film ended and Wayne put his arm around Dotty's waist as he escorted her through the foyer.

"Sorry about earlier," he said, stroking her damp hair. "Are we going for some food?" he asked. She was still cross with him and his apology seemed half-hearted.

"I don't think so, Wayne. I'm not hungry now after wolfing down all that popcorn." That was how she would punish Wayne for his clumsiness.

"How about a drink then?"

"If I'm honest, I'm tired." It was true that Dotty had been tidying the garden at home most of the day so that wasn't just an excuse. She genuinely was done in.

"Can I tempt you to coffee back at mine then?"

"Maybe another time." Dotty smiled.

"Oh, so you want there to be a next time?"

"Yes, that's if you do too." She squeezed his hand and looked him in the eye. How could she resist those alluring green eyes?

"Oh, yes, I'd like to see you again. I'm only sorry with my work commitments I'm busy at the moment. With this murder inquiry, I've been called in on overtime, so it's pants."

They walked hand in hand to Wayne's car.

"I understand. Don't forget, I'm used to a police officer's lifestyle with my dad."

"Of course, how is he doing?"

"He's laid up with a bad back, but he's enjoying his retirement on the whole. He normally does the garden, but he roped me in today. That's why I'm so tired, sorry."

"Not to worry. Another time maybe?" Wayne raised one eyebrow and looked at Dotty.

"Yes, sure. Let me know when you are free."

"Will do. Come on then, let's get you home." They climbed in the car and drove along in silence. Dotty's weariness made any effort to talk almost impossible. Wayne's mind was on his work. He was hungry but he would stop at the Indian takeaway after he dropped Dotty off. As they drew closer towards Dotty's road, she decided to chance her arm.

"How's the case going?"

"We've got a few leads we're chasing up. You've met Evelyn Collins, haven't you? She's very pedantic. Sometimes, because she's so thorough, police time is wasted unnecessarily. I know we must follow up on everything, but she's been around long enough to realise when something is leading nowhere. I suppose it's the right way to go about things. A lot of what we do seems a waste of valuable man hours."

"Millie didn't do it, you know."

"I hear you."

"Do you have any leads?"

"You'll know from your dad being a copper that I'm not allowed to say."

"No, of course not. Do you get on with your boss?"

"Most of the time I want to wring her neck but as she's my boss, I have to bite my tongue." Dotty laughed. She couldn't imagine Wayne taking orders, nor did she like the sound of working with DS Collins. She seemed too serious for Dotty. They pulled up outside her house.

"Here you are, miss. I've got you home safe and sound." Dotty moved to pull on the door handle.

"Aren't you forgetting something?"

"What's that?" She turned to look at Wayne. He pursed his lips.

"Kiss for the driver." She moved towards him and their lips met. They petted, and he went to kiss Dotty's neck. Her body sent ripples of delight down to her toes. If she didn't get out of the car soon, she would crumble and be at his mercy. She drew away. He acknowledged her move.

"Yes, you better go. You're turning me on too much. If you don't go now, I may whisk you away to my lair."

"Thank you for a lovely evening." Dotty smiled, but she wasn't staying for any more kisses.

"My pleasure." He blew her a kiss as she closed the car door. She waved to him as he drove off.

Just as she put her key in the lock, a message pinged through. She thought it might be Wayne saying goodnight or something saucy, but it was from Kylie.

Still no word from Auntie Flo.

Chapter 15

Where was Auntie Flo? Kylie woke up in the middle of the night just as she had every night since the news of Flo's disappearance. Her throat was parched, so she reached for the glass of water on the bedside table. She groaned when she saw the time. It was unlikely she would get back to sleep now. She could kill her auntie Flo for causing all this concern. Kylie wished she didn't care so much but her friends' comments had bothered her. They thought Flo might have something to do with Nigel's death. She couldn't understand why her uncle Chris wasn't doing more to find his wife. She decided to pay him a visit the following day.

"Aren't you getting worried?" Kylie asked.

"She'll come back when she sobers up. If I'm honest, I'm glad to see the back of her. She's been smoking that weed, and it's sending her loopy. She's paranoid that I will leave her. I'm not likely to run off anywhere at my time of life. I mean where would I go? Plus, she's not getting half of my pension." Chris didn't seem to twig to the fact that Flo had spent most of his lump sum and the lion's share of his pension, anyway. He was a mild-mannered man who called in the bookies every morning. After checking the form of the horses, he put a bet on, but he never spent more than a few quid. He also went out for a couple of pints on a Friday night. Up until Flo getting these funny notions selling drugs, he had lived a simple life. He worked for the railways until he was sixty-four and was proud of the forty years that he gave them. His bad heart meant he had to retire early and being under Flo's feet seemed to send her off the rails. She had always liked a drink but over the last few years, it had become a daily occurrence. The pair of them were in denial that there was a problem but when Kylie thought about the fact that Auntie Flo had disappeared like this before, she began to wonder. She would rather her aunt be off drinking herself silly somewhere than be guilty of murder, at least she thought that was the most preferable option.

"Have you no idea where she might be?" she asked her uncle.

"Your guess is as good as mine."

"Don't you think you should tell the police?"

"What, and waste their time? No, she'll be back when she runs out of money, mark my words." Kylie looked across at her uncle and for the first time saw how the lines on his face had deepened. She shook her head. He should be enjoying his retirement, not worrying where his wife was. Uncle Chris shouldn't have to go through all this heartache. Although to be fair, he didn't seem too concerned. The way he sat reading the paper looking content, his mind wasn't on Flo's whereabouts. Chris folded his newspaper and placed it on the table.

"Well, I suppose I better tend to her plants while she's away. There will be all hell to pay if she comes back and her precious marijuana has died."

"Doesn't it bother you the way she is?" In Kylie's eyes, Uncle Chris was a doormat. The softer he was with his wife and the more leeway he gave her, the more she took him for a mug. It seemed like a very one-sided relationship to Kylie, but it wasn't her place to interfere. When her mum intervened a few years back and said something to Flo, they didn't speak for six months so it was unlikely that anyone could change her.

"You know that Auntie Flo was near the soup stall where the source of the poison was found before Nigel took his fateful dose?"

"What are you implying, young lady?" Chris looked over the top of his glasses as Kylie.

"Nothing." She put her hands up in defence. "I don't think for one minute that Auntie Flo is guilty, but she isn't doing herself any favours by disappearing. She had a long-running vendetta with Nigel."

"Everyone hated that man. I'm surprised he had any friends but if you want to know what was going on, you should speak to his closest acquaintances."

"Why, who did he mix with?"

"There's the bank manager, Fred Peterson and that lawyer chap, what's his name? You know the one there was all that hoo-ha about last year."

"Oh, you mean the guy who was nearly struck off for his racist remarks, Julian Cranford."

"Yes, that man is decidedly dodgy. He wriggled out of a court case 'cos he found some loophole in the law, but they virtually proved that he wouldn't represent black people. He's not a nice man at all by all account. No wonder him and nasty Nigel got on so famously."

"Maybe I should pay him a visit?"

"Don't you go getting yourself involved. No good will come of it and you could end up in a whole heap of bother mixing with wrong 'uns like him."

"If it'll help clear Auntie Flo's name then I'll do all I can."

"I don't know, what are you like? There's no telling you, is there? She doesn't deserve your loyalty and your trouble is you're too strong-willed." Chris rose from his chair and playfully ruffled Kylie's short-cropped hair on his way out of the room. She pondered what her next move should be.

Given Uncle Chris's warning, Kylie decided she wouldn't tackle Julian Cranford on her own. If he was slippery enough to get off a court case, then she needed someone like Dotty to assist her, even if it was only for moral support. She had done her homework on him and found out he met up with friends on a Friday night. As luck would have it, she wasn't working this Friday. Now that Graham had got new bar staff in, she was able to swap and change her rotas round. Seeing as she couldn't talk Kenny into having a night out, Dotty would do as a suitable alternative. After they had spoken to Julian, they intended to go to the wine bar. Best laid plans never came off as expected.

Kylie had it on good authority that Julian spent Friday nights at the local social club, so the girls started their evening there. They walked through the door of the single storey building with its whitewashed exterior. It looked more like a working men's club than somewhere a lawyer and a bank manager would meet. An elderly bald-headed man sat in the reception area behind a tiny round table. He had a large A4 size notebook in front of him. A dark blue and maroon coloured scarf hung around his neck over a blue striped jumper and he wore a cap. The girls were about to walk through to the bar.

"Have you got your membership cards, ladies?"

"Membership cards?" Kylie looked at Dotty.

"Yes, you have to be a member to come in here."

"Oh, I didn't realise." Kylie frowned.

"You can join, if you like?" The man looked smug.

"And how much is it to join?" Kylie asked.

"Twenty pounds a year……. each." The man smiled a sickly smile.

"Sack that." Kylie pulled a face. "I only wanted a word with my uncle Julian." Dotty's eyes widened.

"Your uncle Julian?"

"Yes, you must know him, Julian Cranford."

"Ah yes, he's upstairs in a private meeting."

"A private meeting?" Kylie's mouth went down at the edges.

"Yes, his organisation meets once a month up there."

"Oh, you mean the Law Society crossword club, yes he told me about that."

"No, sorry it's the White Brethren Society."

"Oh, of course, silly me. The crossword club meets on Tuesdays. Come on, Dotty. Let's go."

"Did you want me to pass a message on for you?"

"No, it's okay. I'll see him again."

"Shall I let him know who called?"

"It's fine. I'll surprise him." Dotty and Kylie couldn't wait to get out of the clubhouse. They blurted out with laughter.

"Law Society crossword club," Dotty laughed. "That's a new one on me."

"Up there for thinking." Kylie pointed to her temple, "and down there for dancing." She did a jig as they skipped up the road.

"Come on, we'll forget your uncle Julian for this evening and leave him to his brethren, whoever they are. Let's go to the wine bar." Dotty linked Kylie's arm. The girls chuckled. Suddenly, Kylie pulled up and turned to her friend.

"Wasn't Nigel Hastings a member of the White Brethren Society?"

"Now you come to mention it, he was. I saw that name at Judith's place on one of his letters. Could it be significant?" Dotty held her chin between her thumb and index finger.

"Could be. We need to find out more." Both girls nodded.

Chapter 16

Dotty was in a good mood. Tracy Ballantyne, who had a clothes stall at some of the same fairs Dotty attended, messaged her to ask if she'd help out at a charity fashion show she was running. It was an annual event at St Winifred's church hall where the local vicar got involved in the community. He was keen to help promote the local retailers. At first Dotty felt smug, thinking she was being asked to model clothes, but Tracy wanted Dotty to do the makeup for the girls. It was better than nothing. Even though she wasn't formally trained, Tracy must be impressed with the way Dotty applied her makeup, so she still took it as a compliment. She readily agreed. Since putting the date in her diary, Dotty had been going around the various chemists and stores in the area asking for free samples to use at the event. She was encouraged by the amount of support she received from the local folk.

Because of her involvement, she was also given tickets to sell. She did well. Half of the women in her road bought a ticket including her mum and Betty Simpson from across the road. Betty didn't seem the most fashion-conscious of women. She probably wanted to attend to show her support for the charity, or more likely so she could have a good old gossip, Betty's favourite pastime. On the day of the event, Dotty asked Rachel to come along and help. There was plenty to do with several models needing a touch of glamour, so it would be a bonus to have Rachel there. Kylie was into makeup and would have also been a great asset, but she couldn't get the time off work.

Things didn't quite go to plan. They arrived at the allotted time. Tracy looked flustered. She scurried up and down the clothes rail.

"Where's Phoebe?"

"Her train has been delayed." A voice piped up.

"Oh, no, what are we going to do?"

Phoebe wouldn't be there on time now, so Rachel was asked if she minded stepping in to cover for the missing model. She was thrilled. Dotty might have been miffed that she wasn't asked but convinced herself that Rachel was the same size as Phoebe, whilst she was slightly larger.

As soon as she started working on the models, she was in her element as she beavered away applying foundation and eye shadow. A couple of the girls did their own makeup and Dotty added extra glitter powder for effect. Rachel had time for a quick practice before proceedings began and she was a natural. The curtain opened, and the Reverend took centre stage and introduced Tracy and her team.

"I'm sure you will all be thrilled to see what Tracy Ballantyne and her models from Trends on Tap have to show us tonight. I offered to be a model but sadly none of the dresses come in my size." There were laughs from the audience. "After the show has finished, we will have the raffle. Many of the local businesses have generously offered a whole host of prizes." Tracy came on stage and addressed the small crowd who clapped politely.

"Guys, have we got a show for you tonight. The models have all done an amazing job. If you see any pieces you like, they will be available to purchase or order at the end of the catwalk session. As always, this is a charity event so all profits will be shared between helping the local hospice and funds for the new church building. Please give generously."

Once the performance started, Dotty watched from the side lines. The music blasted out. The event was full of glamour and sparkle. She was proud of her friend and she enjoyed working on the models. She wasn't a professional makeup artist, yet everyone seemed impressed with her ability and commented on how good the girls looked. A lot of her tips for applying makeup had been gleaned from the various blogs that she read regularly. Rachel walked on stage and the hit "No Limit" came on. The music whooped the crowd up into a frenzy and Dotty joined the rest of the audience clapping in time with the beat. The finale ended with a cascade of gold paper descending from a large net placed close to the ceiling. It looked spectacular, but Dotty was glad she wasn't the one clearing up the mess.

Tracy showcased all her best pieces and sales went well at the end of the show. Reverend Philip Munroe had done his bit to help, providing some of the refreshments. He walked around telling anyone who would listen about the latest developments for their new building as well as informing them about the restoration work on the existing church. Apparently, the recent floods had highlighted yet another hole in the roof.

Dotty had dressed the part tonight. She looked sophisticated and elegant with her hair up in a French pleat. Her signature style was to wear polka dots, and she didn't disappoint with her vintage navy dress with its full skirt and contrasting white collar and bow. She finished the look off with navy and white peep-toe shoes that now crippled her feet. She hadn't had time to talk to her mum or any friends or neighbours until the show was over. After grabbing a glass of Buck's Fizz, she went over to chat to everyone. Drinks were served and nibbles disappeared off the plates into the greedy mouths of the audience. There were many people attending that she knew, and she smiled as she walked around greeting people.

"Well done," Dotty's mum said, patting her on the back. Out of the corner of her eye, Dotty spotted Betty Simpson walking towards them. Unusually for Betty, she had worn lipstick and a smidgeon of powder on her face. It did nothing to enhance her appearance. Neither did the brogue shoes or thick green tweed skirt and lilac jumper, although for once her clothes looked well-coordinated.

"Hello, Betty. Does anyone fancy a top-up?" Meryl, Dotty's mum asked.

"Another tea would be wonderful and if you can pop me a couple of those rich tea biscuits on a plate while you're there."

"Dotty?"

"No, thanks, mum."

Dotty was left alone with Betty. Sometimes that was a good thing, on other occasions she could be a nightmare and asked too many questions wanting to pry into all the goings-on. One thing was for sure, she was always hard to get away from. Betty spoke into Dotty's ear.

"That was a lovely show, wasn't it, Dotty? The music was very loud, and some outfits were a bit too modern for me but I'm sure the young ones will buy them. You know, there was a time when I was skinny like those girls. Your friend, Rachel looked very nice, didn't she?" Dotty nodded and looked over at the queue around the clothes rail that Tracy put on display. Women scurried around looking for their sizes. Two women grappled over the last fur shrug, but Tracy averted a crisis saying she had more in stock. Rachel was deep in conversation with the vicar.

"How's your investigating going?"

"Not made much headway." Dotty shook her head, "and it's affecting poor Millie."

"It's not fair that Millie should be in the spotlight like that. From what I have heard her soups are nice, and she uses organic produce."

"Oh yes, Millie only uses the finest ingredients." Dotty was keen to show support for her friend.

"Listen, Dotty," Betty moved in closer towards the younger woman. "I'm not one to gossip or talk about someone behind their back but," she looked both ways before continuing, "you know that Edna Salcombe was having an affair with Nigel and that was why his wife kicked him out?" Dotty's eyes turned into saucers, not so much because of the affair more that anyone would want to be with Nigel.

"Are you sure, Betty?" Dotty looked taller than ever next to Betty's short round frame.

"Have you ever known me to be wrong? I spoke to poor Judith some time back in the butcher's shop, out of range of eavesdroppers, of course, but she was beside herself with what to do." Betty's information was usually spot on, and this sounded like it had come to her firsthand. If Betty told you something, it was normally guaranteed to be kosher. Dotty would have to check it out.

Chapter 17

The horn sounded outside Dotty's front door. She checked herself in the hall mirror before buttoning up her raincoat. The dark sky outside threatened to bring along a storm very soon. She rushed down the path and climbed into the passenger seat of Wayne's vehicle. He leant over and kissed her.

"Right, where will it be then?"

"Do you want to try that country pub I told you about?"

"Okay, do you know the postcode?"

"No, but I can direct you."

"Fair enough." He nodded and turned the key in the ignition. The car revved up, and they were off.

They drove through the village and along the highway. At the next set of traffic lights, Dotty instructed Wayne.

"Get in the right-hand lane." Dotty waved her hand pointing right.

"Calm down, there's no need to be so bossy." Dotty frowned.

"I'm only telling you which way to go."

"I've had enough of women telling me what to do for one day." Dotty sighed and remained quiet. If Wayne had a bad day at work, he shouldn't take it out on her. She ignored the altercation because she was glad to see him so soon after the last time. He must be keen, yet something inside made her feel uncomfortable.

They got to the pub, and she ordered a large glass of red wine. Wayne wasn't drinking because he was driving, so grabbed himself a bottle of coke. They took their drinks and sat in the corner of the quiet country pub.

"It's nice in here," Wayne said, looking at the décor with the brass artefacts and black and white photographs of bygone eras hung around the room.

"Yes, I like it. The food's not bad either."

"We should book in for Sunday lunch sometime."

"That would be nice." Dotty smiled. Wayne's previous bad mood had disappeared. "How are things going at work? You seem stressed."

Wayne shook his head and took a long glug of his coke before answering. Dotty couldn't tell if he was annoyed at her question or if something else was bothering him.

"My boss expects us all to jump through hoops. She gets irritated when information isn't forthcoming. You know the type. She wants everything done yesterday. She can be hard work but she's a good copper deep down and she gets the job done I suppose. I shouldn't moan. She's not the worst boss I've had by a long shot."

"Yeah, I've had some ropey supervisors in my time. The difference is your job has a lot more responsibility behind it. I don't have a proper career like you, so I walk out of jobs if someone upsets me." Dotty laughed.

"Believe me, I've frequently thought of doing that but with a mortgage, around my neck, I have to plant my feet firmly on the ground and grin and bear it."

"Does your boss know you're seeing me?"

"I keep Evelyn Collins out of my private life, thank you very much. What I do outside work has nothing to do with her." Wayne's tone was abrupt. It made Dotty wonder if his boss had broached the subject with him.

"How long have you been with the police?"

"It was my first job after college. I was fortunate. They were recruiting at the time, so I took the exams and got straight in. It's not a bad life, and the money is decent."

"I wish I could say the same about my job. Somehow, I don't think chocolate work will ever make me rich."

"Is there anything else you fancy doing?"

"Oh, there are so many things I like the idea of and then I try them and realise they're not for me."

"When you were at school, what did your careers advisor suggest?"

"He said I should do something creative."

"There you go then — you are doing."

"I know but I'm not cut out to run my own business. I'm hopeless at maths, so doing the accounts is a real ball ache."

"That's what accountants are for."

"I may think about going to college and getting a trade or something behind me."

"I wish you luck whatever you decide to do. I'm sure you will be successful." Wayne took Dotty's hands in his and leaned over and kissed her. He hadn't intended it to be passionate, but it ignited a primal desire that erupted and made him continue. Their lips were locked and as much as Dotty didn't like showing affection in public, she couldn't prise herself away. She enjoyed the tingling sensation that now marched around her body.

The kiss ended, and they gazed at each other with longing. Dotty's five-date rule before she slept with someone showed signs of being broken. So, when Wayne asked her at the end of the evening if she'd like a nightcap back at his place, she readily agreed.

They left the pub and ran to the car. The rain pelted down. They both felt the anticipation of excitement at the thought of their bodies becoming as one. Whilst Wayne hadn't known Dotty would be up for a more intimate arrangement, he was glad he tidied up his house before he came out. They drove along in silence. Wayne kept looking over at Dotty and smiling. He winked and held out his hand for her to do likewise. When he squeezed her hand, it was like an electric shock for Dotty.

The rain came down heavier. Dotty watched the droplets as they snaked down the windscreen. This wasn't a night for the faint-hearted. The wind howled through the side window. As they drove back past the dual carriageway onto the country roads, Dotty switched her attention to the changing scenery. The tyres hissed along the rain-soaked ground. Wayne drove on through the wooded area towards open fields. It was hard to see too far into the distance with the mist caused by the wet weather. Few cars drove past to light up their darkened journey. There were no streetlights in this rural part of Sussex. In daylight and fine weather, this was a pleasant run out, but not tonight. This year, spring had been plagued by torrential rain and gale-force winds. Any little sunshine they had, Dotty was out, making the most of it with Winnie.

The car moved steadily along. The shiny grey Volkswagen Passat was Wayne's pride and joy. It was the first time he had been able to afford a brand-new car, and it was thanks to all the overtime from the murder inquiries he worked on. He always said that whatever bad was going on in the world, there was always an opposing positive side for someone. If lots of people died, then the undertakers were happy. Snow was good for the team who got called in on overtime to work on the road gritters. Wayne felt fortunate to have a good job that he enjoyed. He believed he made a difference in people's lives and the only downside was the unsociable hours and a demanding boss.

They turned a corner and suddenly there was a clunking noise. The car bounced up and down then shuddered to a halt.

"Blast." Wayne hit the dashboard.

"What is it?"

"A flat tyre." He looked up at the sky. The rain showed no sign of stopping. He sighed. "Not to worry, I'll have it changed in no time." Wayne hunched up his collar and got out of the car.

"Do you want any help?" Dotty called.

"No, you stay in the warm. There's no point us both getting drenched."

Dotty sat waiting. The rain affected her view outside so she couldn't see the problems Wayne was having. He pulled out the spare wheel and jack. Dotty sat there for ages. She heard Wayne cursing and swearing so she got out of the car to see what was wrong.

"What's up?"

"Spanners."

"Spanners?" Dotty quizzed.

"I took out my spanner set the other day and forgot to put it back in the boot, so I can't change the wheel. This is a disaster. I'll have to call the emergency services. I'm so sorry about this."

Just then a vehicle with its headlights glaring came to a halt after noticing the hazard warning lights on Wayne's car. A tall dark-haired man got out of his vehicle. Dotty's heart melted. He was no stranger to the couple.

"Dave!" Dotty exclaimed.

"Sergeant Lockyear, fancy seeing you here." Wayne didn't know whether to be happy or sad at Dave turning up to save the day.

"What seems to be the trouble?" Dave asked.

Chapter 18

Dave Lockyear was much more of a handyman than Wayne, but Wayne knew the score on the love stakes. He wasn't letting his love rival show any prowess. Dave brought out his full spanner set for Wayne to peruse.

"Here, this one should fit." The two men crouched down to check the tyre. Dotty looked on, the hood of her coat was up, and her hands were on her hips. The rain had eased off slightly, but it still wasn't a pleasant task to carry out in the cold wet weather.

"So, have you two been on a night out?" Dotty hoped Dave's detecting skills weren't all about stating the obvious.

"Yes, we've been for a drink." Dotty smiled at Dave.

"And now when this is sorted, Dotty is coming back to mine for a nightcap." Dotty shook her head at Wayne's comment. She could see what he was trying to do.

"Do you want me to change the wheel for you?" Dave asked Wayne.

"No, run along. I can manage. I'll bring your spanners to work." Dave seemed hesitant to move. "Look, we mustn't keep you from your computer games, or whatever it is you do in your spare time. Plus, it's raining. I'm sure you don't want to mess up your slick hairstyle." Dotty thought Wayne's tone bordered on aggressive.

"If you're sure you don't need my help, I'll leave you two and bid you a good night." Dave bowed his head and returned to his vehicle.

"Get back in the car, Dotty." Wayne waved Dotty away.

"Goodnight, Dave," Dotty shouted but Dave didn't hear. He had already got in his car and slammed the driver's seat door.

It still took Wayne an eternity to change the wheel. Dotty felt sure Dave would have done it in half the time. After the way Wayne spoke to his love rival, she wondered if she had chosen the wrong man. Still, if it was because he was jealous then that wasn't necessarily a bad thing.

When he finally got back in the car, Wayne was drenched.

"Don't you like Dave?" Dotty asked.

"I can't say I'm his number one fan. I mean, the way he idolises his mother and takes her dancing, there's got to be something wrong with him." Dotty thought that was rather sweet but said nothing.

"Still, you were quite curt with him and if he hadn't arrived when he did, we'd have been in a pickle."

"Listen, that was only banter. If he can't handle my manner, then he shouldn't be in the force." Dotty decided not to pursue that line of conversation. The unexpected delay in their journey had affected Wayne's mood, and she felt the tension in the car.

They drove in silence for a while. Dotty was having second thoughts about going back to his place.

"The delay has made us late. Can I take a rain check on that coffee and make it some other time?"

"Of course, so do you want me to take you home?"

"Yes please."

Wayne pulled up outside Dotty's home and leaned over to kiss her. He took her hand in his.

"I'm sorry for being a jerk. I'm not usually so moody. Work has been getting me down lately. I shouldn't have taken things out on you. The flat tyre seemed like the final straw. Will you accept my apology?"

Dotty smiled, and they kissed.

"Of course."

"I hope you'll let me make it up to you and allow me to take you out again sometime."

"Sure." Dotty was having doubts though. She didn't like his moody side. The expression — keeping her options open sprang to mind.

She had other things to think about rather than her love life right now. She did the neighbourly thing the next day and called to see how Judith Hastings was bearing up. Dotty went up to the Hasting's large pre-war semi and rang the bell. When Judith opened the door, she looked like she had been crying. The rims of her eyes were red. Dotty didn't believe it was grief, so it had to be something else causing her woes. Dotty soon found out what.

"Come in, dear. I'm not myself right now. Nigel's death has affected me more than I expected." Judith took an embroidered handkerchief out of her pocket and sniffed into it.

"I'm sorry to hear that, Mrs Hastings. That was one of the reasons I called. I wanted to see how you were and if I can run any more errands or do anything to help."

"You're so kind and thoughtful, not like most of the young people today. I've hardly seen anything of my son, Gordon since his father's death. They were so alike, you know. I still can't believe he sided with Nigel when we split up. Children today are brought up to be selfish and mean, only out for themselves. I'm so glad now we never had any more children." Dotty followed her into the kitchen. Judith quickly collected up the papers lying on the kitchen table but not before Dotty saw her wading through bank statements.

"I was passing and thought I'd pop in to see how you were." Dotty's eyes were still on the paperwork which Judith promptly dropped in her haste to get everything out of sight.

"I can do that." Judith tried to push Dotty out of the way, but Dotty's nimble limbs were too quick for her.

"It's no trouble. Here, let me help you." Dotty saw the red demand letters and she also couldn't help but notice the overdrawn figure on the bank statement. It was obvious now to Judith that Dotty had seen what she was trying to hide. "Is everything okay, Mrs Hastings?" Dotty had been crouched down on the floor, picking up papers. She rose at the same time as Judith.

"No, it's not," she wailed. Although Dotty didn't feel she knew her neighbour well enough to comfort her, her automatic reaction was to put an arm around her shoulder.

"Whatever's the matter?" Dotty helped Judith into a chair.

"I'm broke. He's left me penniless."

"What do you mean? I thought he was an accountant. How could he not be on top with your finances?"

"I don't know and I'm not the best in the world for sorting out things like this." Neither was Dotty if truth be known. She couldn't add up well but if there was money going astray, she may spot that.

"Would you like me to take a look?"

"It's driving me insane. I've been wading through everything and it doesn't add up. There has been money going out each month, eating away at his pension fund. I'm not talking about hundreds, but thousands."

"That seems odd."

"That's what I thought. Unfortunately, the bank can't help me until probate comes through, but they said there is nothing in the savings account. The last I knew there was at least twenty thousand. Where has it all gone?"

"I don't know but a fresh pair of eyes may be what is needed, and I promise you my lips are sealed. This is between you and me. I won't divulge anything you have told me to anyone." Dotty had her fingers crossed behind her back. That promise didn't include her two best friends who she classed as exempt from any confidentiality clause, spoken or otherwise.

Dotty had enough trouble sorting out her own finances never mind a complete stranger's. The two women sat together for two hours pouring over Nigel's accounts.

"There seem to be two separate regular payments going out that you can't figure out what they were for. Is that correct?" Dotty felt she would have done better had Judith not been there. All she seemed to do was confuse things.

"If you say so." Judith sighed. She was tired of this now and if she weren't careful, she'd be having nightmares with all these figures jumping out at her.

"Yes, there are some large payments to the White Brethren Society and £1000 each month to Stargazer Enterprises. Was Nigel a keen astronomer?"

"No, not at all."

"It's a shame you say the police have impounded his laptop. That may have thrown some light on to what these payments were for."

"It's all very strange." Judith shook her head.

Chapter 19

"You better come over and see this." Kylie sat in the café chatting to Dotty and Rachel. She had Chris on loudspeaker.

"What is it, Uncle Chris?"

"She's home and this story surpasses any of her past escapades. You won't believe it."

"Come on girls, grab your coats and finish your drinks. Auntie Flo has surfaced. We'll go and see her."

The sight that greeted them when they arrived at Chris and Flo's place was of a dishevelled forlorn-looking woman. Her sheepish expression did nothing to ward off Chris's anger at her tales of woe.

"Where've you been? We've been worried sick about you." Kylie hugged her auntie.

"Believe me, this story takes the biscuit." Chris shook his head and folded his arms. The girls sat down and waited for Flo to begin. She looked down at the carpet as Chris spoke. "It's a wonder she didn't make the national news. She's made a mockery out of national security." Chris's mouth thinned.

"Why what has she done?" Kylie looked at her uncle.

"Tell them. Go on, tell them what you did." Chris raised his hand, beckoning his wife. His tone was the same as if he were speaking to a small child. Flo's head stayed lowered.

"I've been to France," she whispered.

"Where?" Dotty and Kylie chorused.

"I was in France, so I didn't realise anyone was looking for me."

"France?" Kylie repeated. "I don't understand. How did you get to France? Uncle Chris said your passport was still here." Kylie's hands were on her hips. This would take some explaining.

"It's all very hazy. I can't remember how I got there."

"What, you woke up one morning, and you were in France?" Kylie pulled a face in disbelief.

"Well yes, I came to in a farmhouse in Lille." Flo wanted everyone to go away and leave her alone.

"How did you manage that?" Dotty found this very amusing but tried not to show any emotion. Why would someone go on a trip to France then not be excited and want to talk about it?

"So, come on, you didn't get there on a magic carpet. What happened?" Kylie got more irritated by her auntie's evasion by the minute. Poor Uncle Chris didn't like confrontation, and he stood hovering over the women who sat on the sofa. He kept changing feet, leaning from one side to the other, then he bit his fingernails. He looked embarrassed, knowing what was to come.

"I'd been in the King's Head and I had a few too many. My mate, Victor from the bowls club was there, and he told me he was going down in his car that night to Dover, doing a booze run. I thought it would be fun to go along for the ride with him and his mate, Charles. I didn't think about my passport. They never stopped talking on the journey. Worse than women, they were. You should have heard them going on about Brexit, the weather, football, you name it. I got bored and fell asleep in the back of the car. Apparently, they threw a coat over me. I think they forgot I was there if I'm honest. So, when they went through Customs, the officers never noticed me. The following day, I woke up in a farmhouse. The place belonged to a friend of

Victor's, Pierre. He lived there with his two sons, Henri and Davide. Their home was a right mess. They told me their mother walked out on them, so I stayed and tidied up. By lunchtime, they had brought the wine out, and we all started drinking again. My phone died, so I had no way of contacting anyone. We had to do the courteous thing and stay to sample more of the wine. That drinking session lasted a few days. I'm sorry if you were all worried." Flo's voice was hoarse thanks to too much booze. She kept quiet about her aching head. She hadn't changed her clothes in days and couldn't wait to get in the bath and wash away her troubles. She felt like a street tramp.

"Well, it sounds like you've made a mockery of our country's security system." Kylie's voice was raised now. She was angry with herself as much as Flo for all the sleepless nights she had, worrying about her auntie. All that time, Auntie Flo was having the time of her life drinking French wine, getting sozzled.

"How did they let you back in the country without a passport?" Dotty asked.

"Apparently, they've launched a major investigation at the port how it could have happened. Border protection had seemingly been tightened up, but I slunk into France unannounced. The customs officers interviewed me for eight hours. It wasn't pleasant." If Flo wanted sympathy, then she had come to the wrong place. This group of vultures wouldn't show her any mercy. They'd been too worried, Kylie especially, thinking she was dead in an alley somewhere.

"When will you grow up, Auntie Flo?" Kylie confronted Flo with all the questions Chris should have asked but was too fearful of losing his wife to say anything. Instead, he sat down in the corner and let his anger stew.

"I never meant to worry anyone. I'm sorry. This whole business over Nigel Hastings has got to me. Because I mentioned at one point that I wanted to kill him, the police think I had something to do with it. It has all been very stressful. None of you understands." Flo looked close to tears.

"It's no reason to run off and not get in touch."

"I've been through a terrible ordeal. How would you like it if the police spent forever interviewing you? All I did was get a lift into their miserable country. It's not as though I pinched any garlic or onions or their beastly frog's legs. I won't be going back in a hurry I can tell you." Flo's mouth went down at the edges.

"Your breach of security is the least of your worries. You realise that by absconding, it makes the police even more suspicious. You are probably their prime suspect in Nigel's murder now. It's a wonder your picture wasn't shown on *Crimewatch* as public enemy number one. You've not helped yourself by disappearing."

"How would you like it, being accused of something when you've done nothing wrong?" Flo looked at the others to see if anyone showed any signs of being on her side. She was met with blank stares of indifference mixed with anger. "It's alright for you lot, sat in your comfy homes while I didn't even have a toothbrush." Flo was not going the right way about winning over any of her audience. Kylie flexed the muscles in her fingers as though she was getting ready to pounce. Her hand crunched in a ball. She made the bones crack. Dotty and Rachel watched their friend. They could almost see her blood physically rising.

"What, no toothbrush, you poor thing! You'll have to take one out with you next time you do a runner. That will make you happier and ease your conscience." Kylie couldn't help herself from being sarcastic. She was so annoyed. "I'd do something about removing all those marijuana plants if I were you. The police will be knocking on your door soon to interview you. I don't want to be trailing up to Holloway prison in London to visit you." Flo had expected her family to be more supportive. Instead, they gave her a hard time. She whimpered.

Kylie got herself so worked up over her auntie's behaviour that she couldn't bear to look her in the eye any longer. Uncle Chris bit his lip. He looked at the state of his wife. She looked dreadful anyway but Kylie's comments caused the tears to pour out. Flo's face turned red and blotchy. Kylie was in no mood to express any sympathy for her auntie even with all her remorse. If she didn't leave soon, she knew she would need restraining to be stopped from attacking her. Getting up, she stormed out of the house, leaving Dotty and Rachel trailing after her. The front door opened, and Flo's wailing could be heard in the background.

"What an idiot she is," Kylie said as she climbed into Rachel's car and they drove off.

Chapter 20

Dotty had another date arranged with Wayne. For all he was an over-sensitive soul, he seemed keen, so she decided she would ignore his recent moodiness and give him the benefit of the doubt. He had invited her over to his place for a meal. He offered to pick her up, but she insisted on driving. She wanted to be in control. That way she could leave when she wanted. Plus, if he were cooking, he would be too busy to give her a lift.

His aftershave smelt divine and she blinked at the sight of him in a blue T-shirt. His muscles squeezed out of the sleeves. She imagined him as a white version of the Incredible Hulk and that his top would ping apart any moment.

"You look nice," he said as he kissed her and pulled her into the hall.

"So, do you." Dotty smiled as Wayne helped her out of her leather jacket. Tonight, she had worn a tight-fitting black and white dress which had big red roses dotted about the material. It highlighted Dotty's curves. The pencil style skirt made moving difficult, and it had to be done with grace and poise. The cotton and lycra mix showed no mercy. Dotty would normally have worn her large body-shaping spandex knickers underneath, but they weren't the most flattering. If tonight was going to be the night that the couple made sweet music, then Dotty didn't want Wayne finding out all her body confidence secrets. So, instead, she wore her sexiest lingerie, matching eyelash black lace bra and knickers.

The anticipation of how the evening would pan out made her nervous. She was shown to the sofa of the small cottage. She crossed and uncrossed her legs. The table had been laid with a white cloth and a small posy of flowers in the middle. Dotty was impressed. Wayne fixed drinks for them both then left Dotty while he rushed into the kitchen to tend to his cooking.

"Do you need any help," Dotty shouted.

"No, you relax. I shouldn't be too long. When Wayne returned, he wore an apron that had the words – *do you want to see my sausage* emblazoned across the front. Dotty smiled. It wasn't exactly subtle, but she liked his sense of humour. There was a candle on the table that Wayne promptly lit.

"If you'd like to be seated. madam, your first course awaits." Wayne bowed his head and Dotty took the napkin off the table, placing it on her knee. Wayne brought out two plates of duck liver pate, served with toast.

"I'm impressed. Did you make this yourself?" She smiled across at Wayne sat opposite.

"I could lie and say yes but then I'd come unstuck if you asked me for the recipe. It's Sainsbury's Finest."

"You've gone to a lot of trouble."

"I've got competition, haven't I? If I'm going to woo you, I must put the effort in." He winked at her.

"You're certainly doing that," she said, nodding. "This tastes delicious."

Wayne followed up the first course with lasagne and then strawberries and ice cream. By the time Dotty finished, she was stuffed. Wayne had bought in ready meals because he didn't want there to be any mistakes. He could make one or two dishes himself from scratch, but tonight was not the occasion to be experimenting and showing any lack of culinary knowledge.

"I've enjoyed this, thank you for all your hard work," Dotty said.

"I know I didn't do any of the cooking, but I wanted you to enjoy it, not poison you." Dotty thought what a faux pa that remark was, as she thought of Nigel lying in the morgue.

"How are things going with the murder investigation?" she asked.

"With these cases, there is always so much research to do and people to interview. It is a thankless task."

"Talking of research, if I wanted to investigate an organisation that I can find no record of on the net, how would I go about it?"

"You're not getting involved with this murder inquiry, are you?"

"Oh no, nothing like that." Dotty hoped her facial expression didn't give the game away. She wasn't the best at telling fibs. Even as a child, her mum always knew when she was lying.

"I would try the library or maybe the dark web."

"The dark web?"

"Yes, don't you know about that?"

"Not really, no."

"I shouldn't be telling you about it. It is more commonly used by criminals carrying out illegal activities."

"Sounds interesting." Dotty's eyes widened. She helped Wayne clear the plates away then passed the crockery to him as he loaded the dishwasher. As the door of the appliance closed, he lowered his head and kissed her on the lips. Dotty stared up at him, dazed. She hadn't expected his eagerness.

"Do you want coffee, or shall we go upstairs?" She gulped, but no words came out. Wayne took her silence to be affirmative, and he swept her body up into his arms and carried her over the threshold. They behaved like a couple of newlyweds until they reached the bedroom door. Dotty's eyes glared wide as she saw what lay on the bed. She was greeted with a selection of sex toys from a bad kitty mask to a faux fur animal tail butt plug. There were a set of claws, some cat ears and a leather flogger. She picked up a see-through leopard skin corset and turned to Wayne. He stood in the doorway smiling.

"I've got that for you to put on for me." Dotty didn't want to be a killjoy, and she fancied Wayne, but she had never done anything kinky like this before. Her previous sexual encounters hadn't been very adventurous, so she wasn't sure if she could go through with it, especially if this was their first time. Dotty bared her lower palette, a strange look that wasn't very alluring. "You have dressed up before, haven't you?"

"I…"

"Don't tell me you haven't." Wayne rubbed his hands together. "This will make it even more exciting — a sex games virgin. There's some lubrication in the bathroom if you're feeling shy and want to pop the outfit on in there."

Dotty took the costume and breezed past him. Her heart was going ten to the dozen, and it wasn't lust causing it. It was fear. She locked the bathroom door and put her back to it while she contemplated what to do next. This wasn't anything like she imagined things to be. If she'd had her phone with her, she'd have sent Kylie a text for some advice, but she'd left it downstairs. Kylie was more liberal in the sex stakes, more of a woman of the world. Kylie would know what to do in this situation.

In the end, it was Dotty's body that decided what she should do next. The rumblings in her tummy weren't just nerves. Shooting pains stabbed chaotically through her stomach muscles and she got to the toilet just in time. A rush of brown faeces hit the pan at lightning speed. Her body shivered. She licked her cracked lips and waited for another wave of diarrhoea. This situation wasn't ideal, but Dotty felt it was preferable to the one waiting for her on the other side of the door.

Dotty glanced in the bathroom mirror. She looked deathly pale.

When Dotty finally opened the bathroom door, she was still perspiring.

"Are you okay?" Wayne looked at her, full of concern.

"My stomach is off. I think I better go home."

"No wait, see if it settles." Wayne grabbed hold of her arm.

"I'm not feeling very well. Can't you see how pale I've gone."

"I'll get you a glass of water. It will blow over."

"I'm sorry, Wayne. Some other time perhaps." Wayne held on to Dotty's arm tightly enough to cause a bruise.

"You can't leave me like this. I'm all excited now. You can at least relieve me."

"Let go of my arm, Wayne. I'm doing nothing of the sort. I told you, I'm feeling ill." Dotty's long fingernails pushed into Wayne's skin.

"Ow, you bitch. What do you think you are doing?"

"I asked you nicely to let me go now get out of my way." Dotty's voice went up a notch. She pushed past him and down the stairs. Quickly, she grabbed her coat and bag, not waiting for Wayne to show her out. She didn't like how his tone had changed. She wasn't waiting around to see if his attitude improved. If he wanted his oats, he would have to look elsewhere. As she rushed towards the front door, the waves of pains started up again in her stomach. Nausea clawed at her throat. She tried to force down the bile, but it was too late. Her stomach contracted violently, and she lurched forward spewing up liquid onto the walls. She heaved as the pungent stench invaded her nostrils. She took a breath then another wave came. All the food Wayne had cooked for her regurgitated onto the hall carpet. In any other circumstances, she would have stayed to clear it up but after what just happened, there was only one place she was going and that was home. She opened the front door to leave as Wayne turned up behind her.

"I've left you a present." She pointed at the display of vomit and rushed out to her car.

Chapter 21

Dotty needed some thinking time. She knew she should probably apologise to Wayne but after his behaviour in the bedroom, she wasn't intending to. She took out Winnie's lead.

"Come on girl, walkies." Winnie was at her ankles in a jiffy, wagging her tail. Provided the weather kept dry, they would go on a longer walk than usual. Dotty had a lot on her mind. Thankfully, her stomach felt fine now but the events of last night had left their mark and had disturbed her. She walked with her dog along the pavement then veered off into the fields at the back of their house. They jogged along, Winnie eager to chase rabbits and squirrels. Dotty knew how fortunate she was having the countryside on her doorstep and she made good use of it.

She looked across at the view. It was like something out of a Constable painting. The vast expanse of landscape went on for miles. Each of the paths intertwined with one another yet they all had something different to discover. Dotty related that to her life. She must be careful which path she took. Making the wrong choice now could impact on her future. She had been through enough disasters so far and she didn't want to make any more mistakes.

Picking up a stick, she hurled it into the distance for Winnie. Her mind turned to the previous evening, and she shuddered. She should have listened to her instincts sooner. It had been a lucky escape with Wayne. It wasn't just his penchant for kinky sex that concerned her. He had become quite controlling and aggressive. The warning signs had been there from the first time they went out. He was short-tempered with her then. He apologised and blamed work but if he behaved that way when they first met then it didn't bode well for the future. No, she had made her mind up. She would give Wayne a wide berth and give Dave a chance. He seemed a more homely sort, the type of person you could bring home to meet your parents.

By the time she reached her front door, she knew what she had to do, and that was to dump Wayne. In some ways, it was a shame. For one, he could have been a good source for information but that was no reason to continue seeing him. Dotty took off her muddy boots and bathed Winnie. She got down on her knees and rubbed her dog down with a towel.

"Come on, Winnie. Let's get a drink." Winnie followed Dotty into the kitchen, and she sat at the breakfast bar after making herself a cup of tea. She couldn't meet up with her friends at the café this Saturday as she had a fair booked. Instead, they arranged to go over to Rachel's house for a pamper evening — just what Dotty needed right now.

They all agreed to bring something with them. Dotty prepared some home-made sausage rolls, and she bought a foot spa soak for them to try. She also threw in a few chocolates to sample. Since starting up her chocolate business her diet had gone out the window. She couldn't help but give in to temptation. She hoped more exercise and taking Winnie for longer walks would do the trick and keep off the extra pounds. So far, there was only one way the scales were going, and that was up. She resolved to start again in earnest next Monday.

"So come on, what happened with Wayne?" Kylie couldn't wait to get to the bottom of what Dotty hinted had been an awkward evening. She watched as Rachel poured out wine for them.

"It was awful." Dotty relived the previous evening as she went through the events. Her friends found it amusing.

"It was an omen when you broke down that time and Dave turned up to save the day. What did Delphinia say again about your love life?"

"She said I hadn't met the love of my life yet."

"She may have meant you hadn't been out with him. You should give Dave a try."

"Perhaps I'm meant to end up on the shelf, a spinster."

"Oh, shut up, Dotty. The right man is out there for you somewhere."

"Well, he's keeping well-hidden right now. It's okay for you two. You both have partners."

"Well, you had Wayne until last night, or at least you almost had Wayne." Kylie laughed at her own remark.

"Let's change the subject. Is there any news on our murder investigation?" Dotty sat with her feet wearing plastic socks that contained luxury cream to bathe them. All three girls now had face packs and their dressing gowns on and looked like something from the Mikado.

"I've made an interesting discovery," Kylie said.

"What's that?" It looked strange, the girls talking about serious matters with their faces caked in white clay. It became difficult for Kylie to speak properly as the cream set on her face. She sounded more like a ventriloquist.

"It's about Nigel's friend and associate, Julian Cranford, who we know is also a member of the White Brethren Society."

"Oh, you mean the lawyer?" Rachel mumbled.

"That's right. Well, before he joined that organisation, he was in a group called the Great British Harmony Club."

"What was that, some sort of music group?" Dotty asked.

"No, they claimed to be a patriotic organisation promoting a cleaner healthier greener Britain."

"There doesn't sound a lot wrong with that." Rachel nodded. She thought of herself as a champion for a greener environment and was even considering turning vegan.

"Ah, here's the thing. When I investigated it a bit deeper, it turns out they are a right-wing radical group who practice hateful extremism. Their website and Facebook page were closed down as there was cause for significant concern. They were thought to be spreading hate in their propaganda."

"Really." Dotty started wiping off her face pack. The others did the same. "You're clever how you find out all this stuff, Kylie." Dotty took a face wipe and cleared away the last of the caked gunge off her face. She patted her skin. "Gosh, that feels better."

"My skin's tingling. Is it supposed to do that?" Kylie asked.

"Yes, the minerals will have woken up some dormant cells. They'll be having a good old stretch and pushing onto the layers of your skin."

"You do come up with some barmy statements, Dotty." Kylie shook her head.

"Dotty by name, dotty by nature." Her friend smiled.

"Anyway, to get back to Julian Cranford, once it became public knowledge that he was in the Great British Harmony Club, he resigned. Apparently, he was photographed at one of their protests and I have it on good authority that he almost got the sack from his job over it."

"So, it would be worth speaking to him about the White Brethren Society." Rachel picked up the moisturiser, put a dollop on her skin and passed the jar to the others.

"It may have nothing to do with Nigel's death." Kylie massaged the cream into her neck.

"No, but it would be good to check out his involvement. We may discover why Nigel poured so much money into their funds," Rachel said.

"I'll do it." Dotty checked her skin in the mirror. It looked red, but it glowed. She felt the smoothness of her cheek. "I could pretend to be a reporter and say I'd found out about his membership of the society."

"You be careful, Dotty. We don't know what we're messing with here. We know how he wormed his way out of trouble after making some racist comments." Rachel's brow wrinkled.

"I'm surprised his colleagues put up with him if that's the way he is." Dotty looked down at her phone. A message pinged through.

"Oh, look, guys, it's from Dave. He must have ESP."

"What does it say?" Kylie's head bobbed about.

"He's invited me to attend an art exhibition with him."

"I'd rather run a marathon with no clothes on." Kylie stuck a finger down her throat and made a gagging noise.

"I might enjoy it." Dotty smiled.

Chapter 22

Kylie's findings proved to be very interesting. Dotty arranged an appointment to see Julian Cranford. Although he kept his membership of the White Brethren Society low key, him being a member of the Great British Harmony Club was common knowledge and he couldn't deny it. According to Kylie's research, they had radical views on immigration, and they spread hate. He didn't sound like a very nice man if those were his views.

Dotty wore her black pleated V-neckline dress with a white jacket that was tucked in at the waist. She knew she looked smart because her mum thought she was going for an interview. Thinking of which, if she didn't find work to supplement her income soon, her holiday with the girls was off.

When she arrived at the offices of Boodle and Banstead her heart fluttered wildly. The attractive Grade II listed exterior of the building gave no indication to its modern interior as Dotty walked through the door. Chandeliers hung from the suspended ceiling and modern desks and other furniture were attractively placed on the laminate floor. The small petite receptionist with her blonde hair tied back in a chignon bun asked if she had an appointment. Dotty had given a made-up name but hadn't detailed the nature of her business. She had to remember she was now Paula Pickford. She was asked to sit on the hard, brown leather sofa while she waited for Julian.

Ten minutes later, the tall man walked into the reception area. Julian Cranford had the look of a man who had grown up too fast in his youth. His long spindly legs reminded Dotty of the stick man. If he didn't play basketball, then he had missed a trick. From his lofty height, he could easily have tapped the ball in the net. Dotty watched as he walked towards her. His tailor, if he had one, hadn't done a good job because the arms of his jacket were too short. His trousers were also at half-mast, not a great look for someone claiming to be a professional lawyer. He wore the dull grey pinstripe suit made synonymous by lawyers and he had an expression to match. His crisp white shirt had been freshly laundered and showed off the navy and white striped tie. His look was finished off with rimless glasses.

They shook hands and when he smiled at Dotty, he showed off an uneven set off incisors.

"Please, come this way, Miss Pickford." Julian led Dotty into one of the offices. The design inside was more traditional than the outer offices with wooden panelled walls. Julian sat behind a large mahogany desk and signalled for Dotty to sit on the black swivel chair in front of him. The room was huge, spanning the corner of the building. There was a dark wood bookcase bursting with books and several sets of drawers and cabinets. When they were both seated, he spoke.

"How can I help you today?" He took the top off a fountain pen out and sat poised ready to take notes.

"I believe you were a friend of Nigel Hastings?" Julian frowned. A muscle on his temple quivered. Slowly, he replaced the top of his pen and placed it in the breast pocket of his jacket.

"What is the nature of your business, Miss Pickford?" He sat back with his arms folded. Julian was only in his mid-forties but looked much older. His receding hairline didn't help. He waited for Dotty's response. She scanned the corporate artwork around the room with expensive-looking pieces, tastefully framed and considered her words carefully.

"I'm a freelance reporter and I wanted to ask you a few questions about your relationship with Nigel and the association you were part of." The palms of Julian's hands went down on the desk as he leaned forward.

"I thought you were a client. You've come here under false pretences. I wouldn't have seen you if I'd known you were a reporter. Good day, Miss Pickford." Julian pressed on the intercom, frowning.

"I know about your involvement in the White Brethren Society and also the Great British Harmony Club." Julian sneered at Dotty. His mouth was pinched.

"I've nothing to say to you. Don't you go around printing lies about me. I'll have you for libel, young lady. Now get out of my office." He rose from the chair and pointed to the door.

"You have some rather radical views from what I've been reading. Are your employers aware of the extreme philosophies you believe in? The last organisation you were part of has been banned, I hear." There was a knock on the door and the young receptionist entered. If she was supposed to be the bouncer, her tiny appearance was hardly threatening.

"Miss Pickford is leaving. Please escort her out of the building and get her as far away from me as you possibly can. I have no wish to exchange opinions with her. She has come here spreading lies about me." He turned to Dotty and sneered. "If you publish any of this nonsense, mark my words you will live to regret it."

"It's a free country and I'll print what I want." Dotty now wished she were a genuine reporter who could tell the world about Julian Cranford. She rose from the chair and made her way to the door. Julian pushed her out. Another lawyer arrived to see what all the raised voices were about. Dotty addressed him.

"This man will bring your company down with his radical opinions. I'd be very careful if you're considering continuing his employment with this law firm." Dotty didn't know where that outburst came from. All she knew was she was angry with the way Julian treated her. She was pushed towards the front door and jostled onto the pavement.

Irrespective of Julian's views, she had taken an instant dislike to the man. As she walked up the High Street, she wondered what she had expected to achieve from meeting him. She wasn't sure. It was obvious he was guilty of being involved in the organisations. He hadn't tried to worm his way out or make up some notion that they advocated a greener Britain. Whether any of this had any significance to Nigel's death was another story.

Dotty wondered if she would have the same reaction if she contacted Nigel's friend Fred Peterson. So far, they hadn't found a connection between Fred and the White Brethren Society, but Dotty's hunch was that he was a member too. After speaking to the others, they agreed that the best course of action may be to tackle his wife, Sandra. They found out she had her hair done every Friday at The Hair Studio, so Dotty made an appointment there as well.

Considering she had poo-pooed the idea of being a detective when her dad worked for the police, Dotty now enjoyed all this intrigue and investigating. It made her boring life come alive. The appointment at the hairdresser's the following morning had worked out perfectly as she was meeting up with Dave to go to the art exhibition later that day.

Chapter 23

Dotty was looking forward to meeting Dave, later that afternoon. She was also glad to get her hair done. It was ready for a trim. Her usual stylist, Chantelle might be miffed if she knew Dotty was taking her custom elsewhere. The next time she made an appointment with Chantelle, she would explain the reasons for having to visit another hair salon. Hairdressers got very territorial about their customers, but this was necessary if Dotty were to find out more about Fred's involvement with the organisation.

She walked into the salon and was greeted by a smiling receptionist dressed in black. All the stylists wore black. It was the staple uniform for hairdressers. Each of them had put their own stamp on their style. The receptionist had her hair pulled back in a tight bun and she wore a black T-shirt with chains dangling off it and leather trousers. Her black Doc Martens completed her butch look. She took Dotty's jacket and offered her a seat and a drink.

"Your stylist will be Marie today. She should be with you pronto. Make yourself comfy." Dotty did just that and looked around the salon for Sandra Peterson. Kylie had found out her appointment time by phoning up pretending to be her, saying she had forgotten the time she was due to attend. Dotty had seen a picture of Sandra and unless she had changed her hair colour, no one in the large open-plan bright modern salon looked like her. Dotty flicked through a magazine while she waited, glancing up every so often if she caught any movement in her peripheral vision. There was still no sign of Sandra.

Marie came over and showed Dotty to the leather chair nearest the door. Dotty sat down and swung the chair around 360 degrees. It reminded her of being at the fair and her mind took off, remembering times spent on the waltzers as a teenager. Her, Kylie and Rachel would giggle and scream, and the scruffy young attendant would swing them harder and faster. She was always sick when she came off, but she loved it. Sometimes, they would hang around with the fairground lads afterwards, mainly because their parents disapproved. She recalled the time one of them offered her a ride on the back of his motorbike. She had never seen such a gleaming example of sturdy metal. With endorphins popping and her heartbeat thumping, she got on the back as they drove off into the night. Fear gripped her as the wind hit her cheeks. The guy had no regard for the speed limit as he opened the throttle wide. The ride was exhilarating, yet it was the loss of control over her own destiny that filled Dotty with the most angst.

Suddenly, the front door opened. A breeze blew in and hit Dotty's cheeks. That brought her back into the present and she watched as a middle-aged dark-haired petite lady walking in. Dotty recognised Sandra immediately. Within a matter of minutes, Sandra was shown to a station a few chairs down from Dotty. The black cape was put on Dotty, and she was taken to the sinks for her hair to be washed. She wondered how she could get closer to Sandra. When she was led back to the seat near the door, she came up with her plan.

"Do you mind if we move inside the room more, only I have a crick in my neck. It's very stiff and the draught from the door opening is likely to exacerbate it." Dotty smiled at Marie. Her suggestion worked and she was moved over to sit next to Sandra. They started up a conversation.

"I recognise you, aren't you Sandra Peterson, Fred's wife?"

"That's right. Sorry, should I know you?"

"Probably not. I'm Julian Cranford's niece. I've seen your picture with Fred." Telling lies was becoming too easy for Dotty.

"Oh, I see. I didn't know Julian had a niece, certainly not one who lives in the area. He's never mentioned you."

"I don't see much of him."

"What did you say your name was?" Sandra frowned.

"I didn't." Dotty had to think quickly. When she made the appointment, she gave her real name, but she didn't want Sandra to know that for fear of reprisals. "I'm known by my nickname, Dimples." That was the first thing that came into Dotty's head. What a stupid name, she thought. Her friends would be sure to make fun of her over this but at least she had dimples in her cheeks, so it wasn't so far-fetched.

"I see."

"That was a terrible affair with Nigel Hastings, wasn't it?"

"Yes." Sandra didn't look keen on engaging in conversation.

"They were all a member of that club. What do you think about Fred being a member of the White Brethren Society?" Dotty guessed that Fred was involved too and hoped her hunch would pay off.

"I'm sorry?" Sandra frowned.

"You know, the club they go to once a month."

"Oh, I don't get involved with all Fred's business."

"I'm surprised. I mean they have such radical views. Do you agree with their ideology?"

"I'm not racist but I agree in giving Britain back to our own people and that foreigners should be sent home." From Sandra's comments, Dotty now knew exactly what Fred was involved in — the same organisation as Julian and Nigel. Her blood began to boil at Sandra's insensitive remark. The Asian guy cutting a client's hair two seats down heard the comments and raised his eyebrows. Dotty watched as he picked up speed with his scissors. Expertly he chopped away, but there was now a ferocity about his movement. The pace that the hair disappeared off the woman's head mesmerised Dotty. Whilst she was in awe of his talent, she wondered what was going through his mind listening to their conversation. His client was oblivious to what was happening. She took the cup off the saucer and sipped her coffee.

"Someone ought to change the subject." Sandra's stylist sensed an atmosphere brewing.

"I'm just saying. We're passionate ecologists and that shouldn't be taken out of context."

"From what I've seen of the people in the organisation, many of them are right-wing bullies." Dotty's neck muscles tensed. She was having difficulty containing her anger towards the woman and her beliefs. Thankfully, Sandra's stylist felt the tension between the two women and suggested Sandra move to the back of the salon. Sandra agreed and scurried off, holding a magazine on her knee.

Marie continued to talk to Dotty as though nothing had happened. She smiled and asked how she wore her fringe. By the time Dotty was ready to leave she had calmed down. Sandra hadn't surfaced back into the main body of the room so there were no further confrontations. When Dotty went to pay, the Asian worker came over to Dotty. He whispered in her ear.

"Just for your information, she is racist."

"Sorry?" Dotty looked puzzled.

"Sandra Peterson." He looked towards Sandra and scowled. "Pixie, Sandra's usual stylist was off sick one week so, when Sandra came in, I was asked to do her hair. Sandra went mad. She said she didn't want someone from a different culture doing her hair because they wouldn't understand how she liked it. She shuddered when I touched her shoulder."

"You're joking?" Dotty put a hand over her mouth.

"I'm not and I was born and bred in South London. I have as much right to be here as she does."

Dotty's head was spinning when she left the salon. She couldn't believe people could be openly racist in this day and age. Should she mention anything to Dave when she saw him later?

Chapter 24

Neither of Dotty's parents was home otherwise she may have told them about meeting Sandra Peterson. Instead, she continued to build up a resentment against her for her insensitive comments. She checked her appearance in the mirror, having applied a final coat of lip gloss. She was about to step out the front door when her phone rang.

"Hi, Kylie. I'm on my way out to meet Dave. Is everything alright?"

"I've had a weird phone call from Delphinia."

"Why, what did she say?"

"Well, she doesn't have your phone number, but she asked me to pass on a warning to you."

"What do you mean, a warning?"

"She wasn't precise. She told me that she hadn't seen anything specific but that she had seen a premonition and there was water involved."

"Well, that's old hat. I mean I found Nigel, and she knows that. Who is she trying to kid?"

"She told me to warn you to be careful of what you are getting involved in. There may be something else. She said if you were concerned then you should ring her."

"I'll pass on that one. I won't let her spook me out." Dotty also told Kylie about her visit to the salon and Sandra's behaviour.

"I see. So, all three chums were involved. Anyway, have a lovely time. I thought I'd tell you what Delphinia said. Enjoy your afternoon with Dave and don't do anything I wouldn't do." Both girls laughed.

"That means I can do anything."

"Exactly."

Dotty was on her way to her meeting with Dave. They planned to drive up to London together. She had agreed to drive as Dave's car was in the garage. She smiled at him when he got in the passenger seat and she held her cheek towards him hoping for a peck at least but nothing was forthcoming. They chatted away on the journey up to Dulwich. It was nice to find someone with a common love for art.

"Art and crafts were the only things I could do at school. Everything else I was rubbish at." Dotty kept her eyes on the road ahead as she spoke.

"I was good at art and sports, a strange combination. You'll probably laugh at me, but my two favourite subjects now are cookery and needlework."

"No, it's great for a man to be in touch with his feminine side. You must cook for me sometime. I also love cooking." Dotty felt a warm glow inside when they discussed all the things they had in common.

"I'd love that." Dotty seemed to have the knack of getting men to cook for her. Maybe once she got her own place, she'd be able to return the favour. "So, what sort of things do you like to cook?"

"I enjoy baking. My chocolate profiteroles are to die for."

"You don't look like you eat much of your baking. Do you work out?"

"I do a bit of weight training and I run. I have to stay fit being in the police."

They arrived at the Dulwich Picture Gallery to see the Rembrandt exhibition. Dave had been to the gallery before so could direct Dotty.

"Seen anything of Wayne lately?" he asked.

"I won't be seeing him again and I never went back to his place that night you saw us." Dotty looked straight ahead as they walked up the pathway towards the building.

"Oh, it's nothing to do with me. It's a shame that things didn't work out for you two. I probably shouldn't pry but what went wrong?"

"We weren't well suited. I think we wanted different things. We didn't have as much in common as you and I do." Dotty smiled and linked Dave's arm as they walked in towards the reception desk.

"It's important to find a partner with similar interests otherwise when the lust wears off it will all go pear-shaped." Dotty laughed at that remark. "Here let me get these." Dave insisted on paying, so Dotty said she would treat Dave to coffee and cake in the café afterwards.

They strolled around viewing the collection of paintings which included work by Gainsborough and Reubens.

"Are you any good at art, Dave?" Dotty took hold of Dave's hand as they walked through the various rooms. The way he seemed reticent to have any bodily contact with her, she assumed he wasn't a tactile sort of guy.

"I enjoy painting and I've done a couple of courses. I'm better at drawing. How about you?"

"I'm probably the same. I love to paint and find it very therapeutic but it's only when I joined a night class that I found time for art. We should have a day out in the summer and take our boards and easels and a picnic and do some landscape painting."

"That sounds like a great idea."

Dotty let go of Dave's hand as she went up to have a closer inspection at some paintings. She was totally in awe of the artists' skills and thoroughly enjoyed the outing.

"Thank you for bringing me," she said afterwards as she tucked into a cream scone in the café.

"Well actually, you brought me."

"Thanks for suggesting it. I've enjoyed spending time with you. Maybe we could do it again sometime?"

"Yes, that would be nice. You know how it is with work though. I'm very busy and it's frowned upon if we turn the overtime down." Dotty couldn't tell if Dave was making excuses, and that this was his way of letting her down gently.

"How are things going with the Nigel Hastings case? Have your lot arrested anyone yet?"

"I don't think so. As you know I'm not involved with the murder squad. You'd have to ask your friend, Wayne about that."

"I doubt I'll be doing that. Tell me, if you were trying to research an organisation of right-wing extremists that you couldn't find anything out about, how would you tackle it?"

"Is the organisation legal?"

"I don't know."

"Have you tried the dark web?"

"No, and you're not the first person to suggest that."

"I hope you've not got yourself involved with something you shouldn't."

"No, of course not." Dotty coughed and popped a splodge of cream on top of her scone. "It's a nice place this, Dotty said, looking around.

"Yes, we must definitely come again sometime."

Dotty looked across into Dave's blue eyes and when their eyes met, for a moment she was lost in the ocean beyond them. She had enjoyed the afternoon and Dave's company more than she expected to. Although she knew he was good looking, with their previous encounters they hadn't had the same connection as they had today. She realised now that she had initially chosen the wrong police officer. Hopefully, Dave wouldn't hold it against her and would give her a chance to get to know him better.

"Do you have a girlfriend, Dave?"

"No, I…." Dave looked like he was about to say something then changed his mind. "No, I've not."

"I would definitely like to see you again."

"Good." That appeared to be a very uncommitted response. Maybe Dave wasn't into her at all. She would have to wait and see.

They were still both very chatty on the drive home and Dotty dropped Dave off at the police station. He said that he had things to do before his shift started. Dotty was impressed with his commitment. In fact, Dotty was impressed with Dave all round. She would keep her fingers crossed that he contacted her again.

She drove home with a smile on her face reliving their conversations. He hadn't kissed her, but she put that down to dropping him off outside work. He would no doubt be embarrassed to show affection in front of his colleagues.

The roads were clear as she drove up the bypass. She kept a check on her speed as the winding of the roads began. As she grew closer to home, her thoughts turned to food and what to have for supper. She turned a corner and looked ahead. A man stood in the middle of the road flagging her car down. She wouldn't normally stop but he looked in distress. She pulled up her car along the A272 as she was about to cross a small bridge over the River Arun. He shook his hands, pointing to the water below. Climbing out of the car, she went over to where he pointed.

"What is it? What's the problem?"

"There's a dead body down there by the water's edge." Oh, not another one, Dotty thought. Inside she cringed.

Chapter 25

"Don't look. You don't need to see the body. I've pulled him clear of the water, so he doesn't get pulled out with the current. Can you phone the emergency services?" The middle-aged man wore a raincoat and cap. With his arms extended, he shepherded Dotty away from the site.

"Have you tried CPR?" Dotty asked.

"It's too late, the poor bugger's gone. There's nothing more we can do for him other than inform the authorities."

Dotty climbed down the embankment and looked up at the bridge.

"Did he jump?"

"It's possible, especially as there's no one else about but there is a lot of blood around his throat area."

Dotty made the call to the ambulance and police service and climbed back up to the road to wait for them. She squelched across the muddy terrain. Even though the stranger told her not to look, she couldn't help herself and the sight of blood made her nauseous. She steadied herself against the brickwork. The chap poked around with a stick close to where the body lay.

"I think you should leave that to the police," Dotty cried out. He ignored her. She took in a few deep breaths and gulped. The shock of seeing another body in such a short space of time sent her head spinning.

Within minutes, two police cars arrived. She groaned when she saw who got out of the first vehicle.

"Well, if it isn't that meddlesome woman, Dotty Drinkwater," Wayne said to his colleague. DS Evelyn Collins tutted.

"What the blazes are you doing here?" She frowned. "Might have known you'd muscle in where there was a body involved. You seem to make a habit of it." She plunged her hands into her deep coat pockets then marched down the slope towards the body.

"We think he may have jumped." Dotty shouted after her. She was only trying to help but her comments went down like a lead balloon. She hadn't even looked properly at the dead body.

"This was no suicide," DS Collins called out. "The man's throat has been cut. Get the team down here and seal off the area." She started giving her orders out and Dotty walked towards her car. Wayne pulled her arm back.

"How come you've not returned any of my calls?" he hissed.

"I've been busy." Dotty should have told him she didn't want to see him again, but it wasn't a smart move to make an enemy out of a policeman.

"Busy, my foot. I know your sort. You lead men on. You're just a tease." Two of his colleagues were in earshot of their conversation.

"Wayne, please. This is neither the time nor the place." Dotty's feet shuffled as she checked to see who was listening in.

"We'll need a statement from you. Hey, Sergeant Mason, sort this out. I've got more important work to do than talk to Miss Nosey here." If Dotty was offended by his words, she didn't show it. She wanted to retaliate with something equally cutting but bit her lip. The rage inside her festered though and she would have given anything to have been beamed up away from that scene. She wished she'd taken the other road home. She could kick herself for coming this way, all to save a couple of minutes. At this rate, she'd be lucky to get home before midnight.

From the police comments, anyone would think she wanted to be involved yet that was far from the truth. She longed to be tucked up in front of the TV with nothing to do with dead bodies. The officer took her statement and eventually allowed her to leave.

When she got in, it was a different matter. She couldn't wait to tell her family and friends about what happened. She also went over to let Betty Simpson know the following morning. They had nicknamed Betty *Radio Sussex* because she was such a blabbermouth and Dotty took great delight in passing on any news that she heard before Betty. There was a certain sense of satisfaction in telling her something that she didn't know yet. Word got around about her discovery sooner than she expected. Dave phoned her later that morning.

"I believe you had a bit of excitement after you left me last night."

"You could say that. Word travels fast."

"I hope you're not too traumatised by the whole thing." Dotty thought how different Dave's caring nature was to Wayne's.

"The most traumatic part was bumping into Wayne again."

"Oh dear, it's like that, is it?"

"I've hurt his feelings because I haven't been in touch but to be honest, he seems to get upset about the slightest thing."

"He's a bit of a hothead is Wayne. You probably had a lucky escape, deciding not to see him anymore."

"I wish I'd known what he was like sooner."

"Mm, so, have you heard who the body was that you stumbled upon down by the river?"

"No, is it someone I know?"

"I think so, it's the bank manager, Fred Peterson."

"Oh dear, I suppose his wife, Sandra has been told?"

"She will have been, yes."

"He was a friend of Nigel Hastings, wasn't he?"

"Yes, I believe so."

"Very interesting."

"You keep away, Dotty. Leave it to the police."

"I will, Dave and thanks for letting me know who the poor soul was."

Fat chance she would leave well alone now she knew who he was. The call from Dave ended and the cogs started up in Dotty's brain. The more she thought about it, the more she believed the organisation Fred and Nigel were part of had something to do with what was going on. It was too much of a coincidence. Dave had warned her to stay away from the dark web but maybe it was now time to do some research.

That evening she went over to Rachel's. Rachel was the most computer savvy of the three friends and she had entrusted her bloke, Harry from accounts to help. He was a whizz on computers so came in handy at a time like this. The three of them sat around Rachel's computer drinking mugs of coffee as Harry explained what the dark web was all about and how to access information.

"The internet is a much bigger place than you realise," he said, as the mouse clicked and opened up a site. "What you guys are probably aware of is only a small section of what is out there. There are lots of shady corners lurking."

"So, who would use it?" Dotty asked.

"People who want to hide their true location, people buying recreational drugs. There is a lot of illegal activity goes on and each layer of the dark web get more secretive than the last. It is hard to find out who is behind many of the sites, but it isn't just used for illegitimate stuff. People in closed, totalitarian societies can use it to communicate with the outside world."

"Gosh, it's fascinating." Rachel looked at the screen over Harry's shoulder.

"Do you remember hearing about the case a few years back where a website that was there for spouses who wanted to cheat on their partners was hacked. Their details were put on the dark web so they could be blackmailed to avoid being exposed."

"Wow, it's scary."

"There is now a cybercrime unit to look into cracking down on the dark web's use for child pornography and serious crime rings. Hey, before I enter the site, have you got those tinfoil hats I asked you to make?"

"I thought you were joking." Dotty stared at Harry.

"No, we need to hide our appearance."

"It's like Big Brother is watching us." Rachel shook her head and went to fetch the hats.

She brought out three handmade hats and passed them around and put hers on. Dotty and Harry followed suit. They were like pirate hats and they all looked very strange. Dotty couldn't help but chuckle.

"Why do we have to wear them?" Dotty asked.

"It's to stop us from being recognised. We must tread carefully. It's a minefield entering this area. We could stumble on countries selling arms or anything by mistake and we may find out information it is best not to know."

"Should we be doing this?" Rachel gulped. She found the whole experience rather heavy going and frightening.

"If you want to discover what Nigel and Fred were up to, this is probably the only way. I have to warn you though, we could open a whole can of worms."

"I never liked the dark even as a kid." Rachel bit her finger. The way Harry described it, it felt to Dotty like visiting the ghost train at the fair only scarier. If they were going to discover something that they shouldn't then she was glad the other two were with her. She sat expecting something to jump out and pounce on them any time soon.

It was over an hour later when Harry made the first discovery. Rachel had gone to fix more drinks. She walked back into the room and Harry and Dotty had their eyes glued to the screen.

"Well, well, well. Have you read this?" Harry pointed at the monitor. "I found some information out about the White Brethren Society and it looks like someone was blackmailing them."

"Does it say why?" Dotty's eyes narrowed as she scanned the screen.

"No, unfortunately not, but that might explain those amounts going out of Nigel's bank account."

"Well done, Harry. That's a real breakthrough." Dotty patted Harry on the head. "Now we just need to find out who and why. This discovery calls for a celebratory drink. Come on, let's go to the pub."

Chapter 26

Their excitement over finding out about the blackmailing was short-lived. Harry found nothing else.

A few days later Dotty was strolling down the High Street clutching two large cartons of double cream. She hadn't quite got her quantities right for her latest batch of chocolates and had run out. If there was any left over after she finished the rum and raisin mix, she would use it to go with the fresh pineapple she was also carrying. It wasn't the easiest thing in the world juggling the items, along with a bottle of milk, but she was loath to pay ten pence for a carrier bag. There were literally hundreds of bags for life at home. Even Methuselah wouldn't get through all her family's collection of plastic carriers.

She looked up and walking towards her was the woman she'd been hoping to speak to for some time — Edna Salcombe. Dotty stopped to chat with her.

"Good afternoon, Edna. How are you bearing up after Nigel's death? I hear that you two were very close." Edna's cheeks glowed. A police car drove past at a slow pace. Dotty didn't even notice it. She was too excited about bumping into Edna and hearing what she had to say. She didn't see Wayne's eyes narrow as he clocked her.

"It's been a difficult time but I'm getting through. I just hope they find his killer soon."

"Do the police know that you two were an item?" Edna started coughing and spluttering.

"That's none of your business."

"Oh, sorry, it's just that a few people mentioned it."

"Who? That two-faced woman, Christine Beckley?"

"I don't think it was her who told me." Dotty frowned, looking up at the sky.

"You know it was her who suggested Nigel try the mushroom soup, don't you?"

"Really? No, I didn't know that."

"Yes, I think it's her you should be talking to, not me." With that Edna marched off in the opposite direction to the one she wanted. She walked about a hundred yards before she realised then doubled back on herself.

Well, well, Dotty thought — the plot thickens.

She couldn't wait to tell her friends this new revelation but had to wait until she arrived home and plonked her groceries on the side. She was due to meet Millie later, so she was excited about this new development. It looked like things may finally be moving forward with Christine as number one suspect.

That evening she got ready with all the gusto of meeting a new boyfriend. Edna's news had put a spring in her step. She couldn't wait to get to the pub to see Mille. They met up outside and hugged.

"Good to see you, Millie." Dotty pushed the pub door open.

"You too, Dotty. Your hair looks nice." Millie smiled across at her friend as they took their seats in the corner of the pub.

"Thanks, I had a bit chopped off the other day. Yours always looks fabulous and I love how you do your makeup." Millie's hair was long, dark and poker straight. It glistened in the light.

"Being in the profession helps. Have you ever thought about becoming a beauty therapist? It's good to do work that you enjoy because it doesn't feel like work then."

"I enjoy making chocolates, but it feels like a chore sometimes because it is such hard work. I've always been put off doing beauty because I'm not clever enough."

"Rubbish. If I can do it, anyone can."

"You have to learn all the muscles, don't you?"

"Yes, but it's not difficult. Plus, once you've qualified, the world's your oyster. You could become a makeup artist working in TV or join a cruise line and sail the seas."

"You're making it all sound very tempting. I might look into it, but I'd have to earn money to get through college."

"I worked behind the bar in a nightclub to pay for my course and I was experimenting making my soups back then. It was tough sometimes, getting in at four in the morning then having to be at college first thing. It was okay when it was my turn to be a model and I could lie there and have my back massaged. I'd be snoring away, catching up on my sleep. Half the time, it felt more like a holiday camp." She laughed.

"You are selling it to me, and it would be good to get a qualification. I might just make some enquiries. Anyway, how are you doing?"

Millie was a grafter. She worked as a mobile beautician in the week and supplemented her income with her soup stall. She was a petite young woman with an attractive smile and a perfect figure. Her heart-shaped face and alluring blue eyes made her a hit with the opposite sex but she was a worrier and it showed. Since Nigel's death, she had developed permanent frown lines and was considering Botox even though she was only in her early thirties.

"The police have left me alone for a while now but I'm still not sleeping, worrying that they think I'm involved. How have you been getting on?"

"My friends and I have spoken to a few people and we've made some interesting discoveries about Nigel's private life. If anything, though, the more we delve, the more people come into the equation. There are many out there who wanted rid of that nasty man. We need to concentrate on who had the opportunity rather than the motive. Too many people wanted him dead but not everyone could have put something in the soup. Plus, how did they know that Nigel would have the mushroom soup? That was what concerned us and now I think we have the answer with the news from Edna that Christine told him to try it. Did you make the soup at home?"

"Yes, that's right, and I transported it in a large urn to the event."

"Was anyone else around when you made it?"

"I made it the previous evening. My flatmate, Amy would have been home. Her boyfriend Rick often comes over. He was probably there that evening."

"Did you go out at all that previous night?"

"I had an eyebrow tint to do for Mrs Jones. I was only gone for about an hour. Could someone have got in the house and doctored the soup then, do you think?"

"It's another option that I hadn't considered. Would it be okay to come over and have a chat with Amy?"

"Sure, but as far as I know she had no axe to grind with Nigel Hastings."

"It's not that I suspect her. I just want to run through possible access to the soup and if it was ever left unattended."

"Well, you can pop over tomorrow if you like. I'll let her know you'll be calling."

"Thanks, that would be handy. So, tell me, are you still not seeing anyone?" Dotty cocked her head and looked over at her friend, concern registered on her face.

"I need time to get over Royston. I feel damaged after that relationship."

"If you want to talk about it, I'm all ears." Millie hesitated then sighed.

"Royston plays in a band."

"Oh, I hadn't realised he was a musician."

"They're only small time but he likes to live the rock-and-roll lifestyle."

"I see."

"It wasn't the groupies that bothered me. It was his drinking. He couldn't control it. He always went too far. Finally, when he smashed the bathroom up after a drunken night out, I decided enough was enough. We've split up many times in the past but pulling the towel rail off the wall was the final straw. It may sound daft, but I reached the end of my tether."

"I understand. So, have you had any contact with him since?"

"I've received a few messages from him written in drunken Chinese but I'm not taking him back again. There have been too many occasions in the past where we've got back together but not this time. I've got to the point where I know he will never change so why should I keep putting up with it?"

"Good for you for making the break. It can't be easy."

"No, especially because deep down I still love him. I just don't like him anymore and I don't like the way he conducts his life." Dotty passed a tissue to Millie who wiped a tear away.

"Whenever you need a shoulder to cry on, call me. Don't be alone with your sadness. You've had so much to cope with lately."

"Thanks, Dotty, that means a lot." The friends hugged.

The following night, Dotty called over at Millie's house to speak to Amy. She explained the reason she was there, and that she was trying to get to the bottom of who planted the poisonous mushrooms.

"I hope you don't think I did it." Amy looked over the top of her glasses at Dotty.

"No, of course not but you were home that evening before the event when Millie made the soup. Could anyone else have had the opportunity to plant something in the batch?"

"Let me think back," she frowned. "If I remember rightly, Rick didn't come over that night because he had a darts match. I've stopped going to watch him. I find it so boring."

"Can you remember if anyone called?"

"I'm certain that was the night that Royston turned up drunk while Millie was out. I shooed him away and wouldn't let him in."

"Could he have got in any other way?"

"I don't think so but, wait a minute, you're right, we don't always lock the patio doors at the back. I suppose it's possible he could have sneaked in."

"I need to pay Royston a visit."

"You be careful, Dotty. Royston can be an unpleasant character, especially if he doesn't like you."

Chapter 27

Royston agreed to meet Dotty at the pub just off the High Street. There was a public carpark close by and at that time of night, there was no charge. Dotty was watching her spending, trying to put a small amount away each month for her holidays. She'd saved all of thirty pounds so far. The carpark was busy, but Dotty found a spot. She got out of her vehicle and weaved through the parked cars and made her way to the corner. This time, she saw the blue and yellow police car prowling along the road. She also noticed who was inside it and her stomach lurched.

She recognised Wayne immediately. It was hard to miss his blond hair. Hopeful that he hadn't noticed her, she kept her head down. It didn't work. She heard a car door bang and footsteps marching towards her.

"Dotty!" She carried on walking, picking up pace. "Dotty!" Wayne was gaining on her. She ignored the cries and continued on her journey.

"Are you deaf?" A hand went on her arm and jerked her body around. She had no option but to stop and face him. Her head worked overtime thinking up an excuse why she hadn't been in touch and why she ignored his calls. She should have been straight with him rather than avoid talking to him, but part of her was slightly afraid of him.

"What do you want?" she frowned.

"Meeting your new fella, are you?"

"I am meeting someone, but it's none of your business."

"I'm making it my business." He stood with his arms folded blocking her path.

"What's the matter with you, Wayne? You're going to make me late."

"I could take you in for questioning for interfering in police work."

"Oh, don't be such a jerk. You wouldn't do that."

"I saw you talking to Edna Salcombe the other day. Don't think I don't know what you're up to."

"Are you stalking me, Wayne?"

"No, just going about my duties."

Just then his colleague arrived, a tall, broad-shouldered copper with dark hair, of a similar age to Wayne.

"What seems to be the trouble?"

"I've just had to give this citizen a friendly warning. It's nothing I can't handle." Wayne hoped his partner would disappear, but he made no moves to go, in fact, none of the three moved. It was like a stand-off. They all stared at each other. Finally, Wayne's colleague spoke.

"If you're all done here, we've got other pressing business to attend to. Come on buddy, let's get out of here. Good day miss." Wayne followed the other officer back to their car. Dotty watched them go. She sighed heavily. That was a lucky escape.

Her heart was still fluttering when she walked into the pub for her rendezvous with Royston. She hadn't met him before but had seen his photograph on Facebook, so she could easily make him out by his unusual hairstyle. It was blond and tousled with a quiff. He stared at her as she walked towards him. He had the strangest expression on his face. It looked more like contempt than a friendly greeting. Whatever it was, it shocked Dotty and made her blush. She stumbled into the leg of a chair. Someone behind her giggled. Dotty ignored what happened and brushed her dress down. Royston glared.

"You must be Dotty." His laugh was a sick sounding gurgle.

"And you are Royston." Dotty tried to force a smile but already felt uncomfortable.

"It's probably not a good idea to be seen with me."

"Why's that then?"

"Haven't you heard?" He smiled briefly then his face turned more serious.

"Heard what?"

"I'm trouble." Dotty gave out a nervous little laugh. Royston's eyes seemed to penetrate her soul. She tried to ignore his stare and looked down when she spoke.

"Have you seen anything of Millie lately?" Dotty asked. Even though she wasn't looking, she could feel the intensity of those dark brown eyes.

"You know the answer to that. You haven't come here for her leftovers so what is it you want?" Dotty gulped and glanced sideways. His face looked mean, almost as though he had the word dangerous tattooed on his forehead.

"You called to her house the day before the Spring Fair."

"Did I? I don't remember. I was drunk."

"I think you do remember."

"Ooh, look at you, all brave and masterful. I like a woman with spirit," he mocked. Dotty ignored his remark.

"Well?"

"You know that's why we split up. Millie thinks I drink too much." At that, almost to prove a point, he took a large glug of his pint. Dotty sipped her drink and watched him. She put the glass down and he grabbed hold of her wrist. It made her jump. "Have you ever been to hell?"

"Sorry?" Dotty frowned.

"I've been to hell and back and I don't recommend it." He laughed. It dawned on Dotty that Royston had already had a few scoops too many.

"I hear you have a bit of a temper." Dotty was chancing her arm now.

"I've given up trying to be good. It doesn't work. So, tell me, Dotty, what do you want from me, a murder confession? I'm not the most pleasant of people to be around right now."

"You know Millie has been interviewed over Nigel Hasting's death?"

"Yeah, the poor cow." He took another large slurp from his glass.

"Did you have anything to do with putting those poisonous mushrooms in her soup?" Royston's laugh grew louder.

"Not very subtle, not very subtle at all," he tutted, staring at his pint. "So, that's why you're here. You think I did it. I can't even boil an egg never mind make mushroom soup." At that, he grabbed hold of Dotty's hair and pulled it back.

"Ow, you're hurting me."

"Don't you come near me making false accusations like that, lady. You stay away from me or you'll wish you'd never been born."

Dotty didn't need any other excuse to get out of there. She had seen and heard enough of Royston. As she left the pub, she shook her head. What could Millie have seen in such a monster? Thankfully, she had arranged to meet Dave at the next bar up the High

Street. She rushed along the pavement, glancing over her shoulder to make sure Royston wasn't following her.

She walked into the modern bar and saw the back of Dave's head. Immediately, she breathed a sigh of relief. He remained seated when she strolled over and kissed his cheek.

"Do you want a drink, Dave?" she asked. Dave declined and didn't offer to get hers, so she went to the bar. She needed a stiff drink after her previous encounter, but she was driving so any ideas of a double vodka would have to wait for another time. She glanced at her handsome partner and smiled. He looked even nicer than usual in his tightly fitted T-shirt and skinny jeans. The man at the next table gave Dave a doe-eyed look, and Dave blushed. Dotty thought that was sweet. She re-joined him.

"I just bumped into Millie's ex, Royston in the King's Arms. What a horrible man he is."

"Oh, what were you doing in the pub?" Dotty felt her cheeks glow. She couldn't let Dave know she was meddling in police business.

"I went in to see if they had any jobs going. I could do with some extra money."

"And did they?" Dave pursed his lips in thought.

"Did they what?"

"Have any jobs?" Dave frowned at Dotty's lack of concentration.

"Err, no, not right now." The way the little white lies rolled off Dotty's tongue was becoming something of a habit but when she thought about it, she may enquire about work there. She could do with some extra money if she were going away with the girls. They hadn't booked anything yet, so there was still time to get her act together and get saving.

"So, how are things with you? You look a bit stressed." Dave was too perceptive for his own good.

"I'm worried about money. I'm skint right now and need to be earning more. My problem is I'm too fond of spending it." She laughed and gazed into his eyes. She wished he would lean over and kiss her. "Plus, I had a nasty encounter with Wayne earlier. He wasn't very nice to me."

"Do you want me to have a word with him and tell him to leave you alone?"

"No, if you get involved, that will probably rub him up the wrong way. You know what he's like."

"Okay, but the offer is there."

By the time Dotty went home, she felt totally miserable. She should have left her car at home so she could have had a few drinks and a bit of a blow-out. Bumping into Wayne had affected her, so had her encounter with Royston. She was about to go up to bed when she stopped in her tracks. Something had struck her. She wanted to dismiss it, but it was hard to forget what Delphinia had said. She told Dotty that she would have a problem with someone whose name began with the letter R — of course, Royston.

Chapter 28

Another day, another dollar. Dotty woke up feeling refreshed and now glad she hadn't got drunk the previous evening. Part of her was upset that Dave still hadn't kissed her. Maybe she would have to make the first move. She wouldn't let Wayne's words deter her from what she needed to do. It was time to call and see Judith again. Dotty still had one or two questions to ask and she wanted to see Judith's reactions when Dotty told her about the blackmailing. Judith was as charming as ever.

"I'm glad you didn't bring that mongrel with you this time."

"Winnie isn't a mongrel. She's a poodle with a pedigree."

"Whatever. Take your shoes off before you come through. I don't want muddy footprints trampling through my hall." Dotty did as she was told. Judith's mood has changed since the last time they met. Dotty decided she preferred the tearful version to the grouchy person stood in front of her.

"I've some news about Nigel's finances."

"Oh, do sit down, dear but take your jacket off first. I don't want mud getting on my sofa. I've only just had it cleaned." There was no mud on Dotty's green Barbour jacket, but she obeyed the woman, after all, it was her house. Dotty coughed, feeling parched. A drink would have gone down a treat, but Judith didn't offer.

"As I say, my friends and I have been doing a bit of delving and have found out some very interesting facts."

"Hurry up, dear. I've got my bridge club in half an hour." Judith looked at her watch.

"It seems that Nigel or at least the organisation he belonged to was being blackmailed."

"Blackmailed? Oh gosh." Judith put her hand over her mouth. "Who by?"

"We don't know that yet. I wondered if you had any ideas who it could be." Judith frowned and looked up at the ceiling.

"Why would anyone want to blackmail Nigel?" Dotty thought there were a few reasons, such as his affair with Edna, but she kept her lips sealed for now.

"Your guess is as good as mine. It was the White Brethren Society that was being blackmailed and Nigel appears to have been funding them. We know his friends Fred Peterson and Julian Cranford were members of that organisation. I just wanted to ask you what you knew about them?"

"Fred was also found murdered, wasn't he? Golly, so you think there's a connection?"

"It's beginning to look that way. Have the police spoken to you about it?"

"No, they haven't said a dickey-bird. It's all very intriguing, my my." She shook her head.

"Did Nigel ever talk about the group?"

"No, Nigel never spoke about anything to me. He was a closed book. The only thing we had in common was our interest in all things horticultural. He had his friends and I have mine. When I think about it, I didn't know half of what went on in his life."

"But I hear you broke up over him seeing Edna?" Judith's face turned a puce colour.

"That woman is incorrigible. She had a nerve. She was as nice as pie to my face, the two-faced hussy." Judith pulled an expression like she was chewing a lemon. It seemed to Dotty that all these women were as bad as each other, gossiping about one another behind their backs.

"I need to ask you something." Dotty thought for a moment, choosing her word carefully. "When you looked after Millie's stall for a short while, did anyone approach the stand?"

Judith shot Dotty a dirty look.

"You believe I put something in the soup, don't you?"

"No, not at all." It had crossed Dotty's mind, but she wasn't about to accuse Judith. "I just wondered if you saw anyone else who may have had the opportunity?"

"The police have also been here asking me all these silly questions. It's all very well for someone to add poison to the soup but how the blazes did anyone know Nigel would ask for it? I didn't know. I hadn't even seen the rotter since our day in court over the divorce. It wasn't good for my blood pressure, so I stayed well away from him. No, it did me no good being in his company, no good at all." She shook her head and Dotty thought she had a point, but she still hadn't answered her question.

"So, did anyone else approach the stand?" Dotty repeated.

"All you need to know is it wasn't me who did it. I wasn't jealous of Nigel even if he made me look a fool. I was the laughingstock of the village — the only one who knew nothing about what was going on for ages, by the sounds of things. In fact, now you've come here telling me all this about his life, I didn't know Nigel at all." She shook her head. "All this debt he left me with. It's like he's punishing me from the grave." Judith was more bothered about the money than catching Nigel's killer.

Judith still hadn't answered Dotty's questions and her stomach quivered as she asked one final time.

"So, no one else approached the stand while you were minding it?"

"No, for the millionth time, no one." Dotty left the woman in peace with just one thought on her mind. Judith Hastings couldn't count.

Later that evening, Dotty attended the first night of Christine's plant food course. She had persuaded Rachel to come with her which wasn't hard. Rachel was on the verge of turning vegan. She recently went vegetarian and said she felt so much better for it. Kylie was another matter. She wouldn't be talked into healthy eating. The idea of eating nuts and seeds made her want to puke. The only way she would eat nuts was in a chocolate bar. Strawberry gateau was about as healthy as she could muster. She didn't mind eating fruit, so long as it was in a cake.

Dotty picked Rachel up. Her face beamed with happiness and Dotty didn't think it was because she would learn about beans and lentils. She waited for her friend to tell her. Rachel couldn't contain herself and had the words out before she fastened her seat belt.

"Harry's moving in with me."

"So soon."

"I know we've only been seeing each other a short while but when you know, you know. I see him every day at work, and I feel we really connect. He asked me, and I was delighted. We're picking all his stuff up at weekend."

"Well, I hope everything goes well for you. He's a nice guy and you deserve to be treated well after the way your ex-husband behaved."

"Yeah, I'm well shut of that no-good cheat and I've never felt happier." Rachel's face bloomed.

They got to the garden centre where the event was taking place. There were about a dozen other women there and two blokes. The girls were shown to the back room, and they took their seats. Everyone politely clapped when Christine introduced herself and read out her achievements which included a master's degree in culinary techniques in plant-based ingredients. Dotty thought what an obscure course to do. She couldn't understand why she deserved a clap for that, but she reluctantly tapped her hands together.

"Tonight, I will outline the course content and explain the basics and principals of plant-based dietary requirements." Christine stood in front of a whiteboard and wrote up a few notes.

Everyone busily copied down what she said so Dotty followed suit.

"Psst, my pen's run out. Have you got a spare?" She nudged Rachel who passed one to her. By the end of the evening, Rachel had written several pages of copious notes whereas Dotty's didn't even fit on one page. Rachel tucked her pad into the large holdall she brought.

Dotty nudged her and whispered, "I'll have a word with Christine."

Rachel's eyes widened, and she nodded. Two other women hung around to speak to Christine. Dotty waited until they finished then approached her.

"I enjoyed that, Christine, thank you. I'm glad you suggested that I attend."

"Yes, your friend seemed to get a lot out of it as well."

"Oh yes, Rachel is into plant food. By the way, I bumped into Edna Salcombe the other day."

Christine was packing her stationery away. She looked up at Dotty.

"Oh?" She anticipated more was coming.

"She said that you were the one who encouraged Nigel to try the mushroom soup."

"Did she now." Christine's mouth narrowed. She continued packing her bag, trying to keep her cool.

"Is that true?" Christine stopped what she was doing and stared at Dotty. Unable to contain herself anymore, she spoke in a raised voice.

"That woman is a nasty, vindictive jealous trollop. She never liked how close Nigel and I were." Some of the class who hadn't yet left, turned around when they heard Christine's outburst.

"So, was it true you mentioned it to him?"

"I may have done. I can't remember. It wasn't as though he could have eaten any other variety anyway."

"Oh?"

"He was vegetarian, you see. The other soups on sale all had meat in."

"I see." Dotty nodded and left Christine to finish packing away.

Chapter 29

Dotty and Kylie met at the Strawberry tea rooms for their weekend treat. Rachel couldn't make it because she was helping Harry move into her flat. Bernadette had recently taken over the running of the café after her mum took ill. Together with her two sisters, they had given the place a new lick of white paint. It already looked spotlessly clean but touching up the paintwork to go along with the pink interior, gave it that extra pizazz. Bernadette was keen to try some new ideas so brought over a sample of salted caramel and cappuccino cheesecake.

"So, you like the shortbread base?" Bernadette asked.

"It's sublime," Dotty's eyes were closed as she licked the spoon slowly.

"I've died and gone to heaven." Kylie swooned. She gave the thumbs up to the new manager who stood behind the counter with her two sisters who also worked there. They had been waiting for the verdict and they all smiled. That was the feedback they hoped for. Bernadette's ambitious new menu was to be let loose on the public the following week, so this early approval was a good sign.

Her and her sisters, Michaela and Rose didn't intend to make any major changes. Michaela hadn't finished her cake making course at college yet, but when she did, the girls hoped to make more wedding and celebration cakes to order. Rose wasn't formally trained in catering, but she had done a business course. They had some big ideas for expansion. Their mum ran the place for seven years and it had a steady stream of loyal clientele who the new team didn't want to lose. They intended to break them in gently with their new products and recipes.

Kylie poured her and Dotty a coffee out of the cafetière they shared. Her movements were short and jerky like she had something on her mind. Dotty couldn't help but notice her friend's unease.

"Is everything okay, Kylie?" Dotty asked. Kylie took a large gulp of air in and went searching in her handbag. She bit her lip and wouldn't look at her friend. "What is it? What's wrong?"

"I've got a confession to make." The tone of her voice lowered. All the quick-witted banter had disappeared. Dotty had never seen Kylie look so serious.

"Oh."

"I've something here for you." Kylie passed an envelope to Dotty.

"What is it?"

"Open it and see."

Dotty tore open the grey envelope and inside was a voucher for a spa treatment. She frowned.

"What's this for? It's not my birthday."

"No, it's a peace offering."

"Why? What have you done?"

For a horrible minute, Dotty thought Kylie had slept with Dave behind her back. If that was the case, then a measly spa voucher wouldn't compensate. She waited. Dotty now felt as anxious as Kylie whose movements hadn't calmed down. Kylie tapped on the side of the coffee mug. She took an eternity to answer. She cleared her throat and adjusted her sitting position.

"I… I don't think I better accompany you to any more fairs," she stuttered. Kylie still avoided eye contact with her friend.

"Why not? What's wrong?"

"Your chocolates are so nice that when you leave me alone with them, I can't stop eating them. I'm addicted to chocolate. You think you've been doing well with sales when all the while, the reason they are disappearing is because I've been eating them all."

"Oh, I see." Dotty was secretly relieved. She had imagined Kylie coming out with something far worse.

"Will you forgive me?" Kylie looked across at her friend. "It's been bothering me because I know it hasn't just been one or two chocolates that I've helped myself to. I just can't resist when I'm near them. I'm sorry, Dotty."

"You're like that around men as well." Both girls laughed. The atmosphere improved. "An interview with you would make a good advert for my chocolates."

"So, are we okay?"

"Yes and thank you for being honest." Dotty was rubbish with her finances so would never have worked out that her outgoings and incomings didn't tally. She spent almost as much on ingredients as she made from the finished chocolates and hadn't realised. "Come here." Dotty beckoned Kylie towards her and they hugged.

"What are you like, you munchkin?" Kylie sipped her coffee, thankful that her friend hadn't gone mad.

"Have you heard any news about how the police are getting on with Nigel or Fred's murders?" she asked her friend.

"No," Dotty shook her head. "Wayne has warned me about getting involved and Dave doesn't seem to know much or if he does, he's not letting on."

"How about your dad? Does he still get to find out police business?"

"To be honest, since he retired, I don't think he gives a monkey's. He's happy pottering around the garden and playing golf and he stays out of everyone's business."

"Who is still in the frame?"

"Well there's your auntie Flo but I doubt she's capable of murder. She can't even look after herself, never mind kill someone."

"I agree. She's a hopeless case and I believe she was in the beer tent before she walked over to Millie's soup stand."

"Why doesn't that surprise me." Dotty laughed.

"Christine has to be the number one suspect now. She knows all about mushrooms, she had motive because she was jealous of Nigel getting with Edna and she suggested for him to have the mushroom soup."

"But if it was Christine who killed Nigel then why would she also kill Fred Peterson?"

"Maybe he found out what she had done, or it could be someone else who killed Fred."

"So, you don't know if the police found any clues at the scene?"

"I didn't hear anyone mention anything when I was there, and I didn't see anything such as the knife. I wasn't looking though. It came as a surprise when DS Collins said he'd been stabbed."

Just then, Kylie's phone rang. She saw who it was and put it on loudspeaker for Dotty to hear.

"Hello, my darling. Delphinia here. Listen, I'm sorry if you feel I'm pestering you, but I've been getting some bad vibes about that friend of yours, Dotty." Both girls looked at each other, their eyes wide open. Kylie muted the loudspeaker and passed her phone to Dotty.

"Hi, it's Dotty here."

"I don't want to worry you, but I keep having visions and I fear that unless you stop your involvement in the work you are doing looking into the murder, then something bad will happen to you. Please leave well alone."

The call terminated and Dotty turned to Kylie.

"I'm not sure what to make of that. Delphinia is warning me to stay away but the more I think about it, the more I am suspicious of her. Her tent was close enough to have sneaked over to Millie's stand. She is more than competent at knowing about potions and their effects, plus she didn't like Nigel. Rather than her sending me a warning to keep away, she has made me keener to delve deeper."

"Yes, I wouldn't mind finding out what she knows about the White Brethren Society." The two girls looked at each other and nodded.

In the end, it was Harry who beat them to it.

Chapter 30

Dotty's cab pulled up outside her house and the taxi driver beeped his horn. She glanced in the hall mirror, gave her hair a quick pat, and rubbed her lips together to make sure her lipstick was just right. Grabbing her jacket, she shouted out to her parents.

"I'm off."

"Have a nice night," her mum replied. Dotty slammed the front door shut. She was meeting Dave again. They were meeting at the wine bar without their cars, so they could both have a drink. It had been Dotty's suggestion. She hoped that by loosening him up a bit, it would give him the courage to become more intimate with her. He was just the opposite to Wayne. Wayne couldn't keep his hands off her and whilst she preferred Dave's gentlemanly conduct, it had gone on too long now. If he didn't make a move on her soon, then she would make designs on him. That is once she had slurped a few shots and a few glasses of prosecco.

As always, things didn't go to plan. Dotty drank too quickly. She had a thirst on her like she'd been stranded in the desert for a week without water. She guzzled the wine was like she was in a drinking competition and had to finish first. Nerves got to her. She'd had enough of waiting. At one point, she grabbed hold of the collar of Dave's rugby shirt and pulled him towards her, trying to go in for a kiss.

"Whoa, steady on, girl." He gently unfolded her hands off the material and pushed her away. She sat back on the hard leather chair and sighed. "Are you okay, Dotty?"

"I've had too much to drink."

"You will have a sore head in the morning." Dave laughed. They chatted some more. Dave seemed oblivious to Dotty's plight, trying to woo him. Because she had been sat down most of the evening, when she came to stand up, she was unsteady on her feet. When it was time to leave, she wobbled across the carpet, linking Dave's arm.

The cool night air hit her as they opened the door to walk outside. She staggered along the pavement then stopped. Dave turned to look at her just as her mouth opened and the most putrid smelling liquid came out. Vomit splashed onto the ground and over his new jeans. He hailed a taxi and gave the driver her address and the money to get her home safely.

The next morning, the only thing Dotty remembered about the evening was the sight of Dave's face when she was sick over him. He didn't look too pleased. She would have a lot of grovelling to do if she wanted to see him again. For now, she reached for the painkillers to ease her pounding head and felt totally sorry for herself.

Rachel phoned Dotty that evening to give her an update on how the move had gone. She sounded upbeat. After recounting her own weekend's escapades, she asked Rachel about hers.

"Was it horrendous, getting all his stuff in?" Dotty asked.

"It's not that, we don't know where to put everything. We'll have to buy another wardrobe. Anyway, we've got some other news."

"What, you're not pregnant, are you?"

"No, silly, it's nothing like that although we are getting a parrot."

"A parrot?"

"That's right. Harry is an animal lover, and you're not allowed cats and dogs here under the lease agreement. I have checked the paperwork and you can have budgies and the like."

"You'll have to watch it with a parrot."

"What do you mean?"

"That you don't give all your secrets away."

"I have no secrets."

"Well, make sure the parrot isn't around when you're making love. You wouldn't want it to pick up on whatever you call Harry in moments of passion."

"You mean like hunky drawers and donkey dude." They both laughed.

"Something like that, yes."

"No, the reason I wanted to speak to you, as well as to catch up, was to tell you what Harry's discovered."

"And what's that?"

"Well, he was working on his laptop earlier. You know what a geek he can be sometimes?"

"Yes."

"And he came across some information that may be of interest to us."

"Go on." Dotty felt a lightness in her chest. Her senses were heightened.

"He's found out who is behind Stargazer Enterprises."

"What, the organisation that Nigel paid out large sums of money to?"

"The very same."

"Is it someone we know?"

"It's Delphinia."

"Wow, very interesting. Well done, Harry." Then in a voice mimicking a parrot, she said, "Who's a clever boy." They both laughed.

"So, do you think Nigel paid to have his fortune told?"

"He can't have paid for that much worth of advice. I wonder what she did for him for that price?"

"Well, he got his oats off Edna, so I doubt it was for services rendered." The girls chuckled.

"Could she have been blackmailing him for some other misdemeanour, do you think?"

"It's worth looking into.

"Do you think she killed him?"

"It's possible. Maybe he stopped paying her. I could check with Judith if the payments ended. Plus, her tent wasn't that far away from where he was killed."

"What about Fred Peterson? Could she have murdered him also?"

"We can check if she had an alibi. If he took over the finances of the White Brethren Society, he may have told her she was getting no more money."

"That's a possibility because he was a bank manager. You may be onto something there."

"What are we going to do?"

"Let's get her over to give us another reading."

"Won't that be dangerous?"

"If she's as good as she says she is and can see into the future, she'll know to expect it."

Chapter 31

Dotty tossed and turned in the night. Pictures of Delphinia flashed into her thoughts. The West Indian lady morphed into an African witch doctor. Dotty dreamt that she cast a spell over her. In the dream, Rachel was banished out of the country and couldn't get back in to see Harry. Dotty was glad when the alarm sounded the following morning.

The girls told Kylie about Harry's discovery the previous evening.

"I can't believe it," Kylie said. "We need to organise another meeting with her."

Dotty felt the adrenalin rush through her body at the anticipation of confronting the fortune teller.

Meanwhile, she had a busy day ahead. She had lots of chocolates to make for a fair at the weekend. She rolled out of bed and jumped in the shower. Her mind worked overtime. Last night, when she eventually got off to sleep, she had convinced herself that Delphinia was behind the murders. The girls had to tackle her before she did any more damage, but they would have to be careful. If she had used a knife to slit Fred's throat, then she was a dangerous woman. Before they made any accusations, they needed to find out where she was the night Fred was killed.

Dotty got dressed and put her apron on. There was no time for breakfast this morning. She had a lot to do. Coffee and dipping into her ganaches would keep her going. The morning flew by. Her mind wasn't on her work though. By lunchtime, she couldn't stop herself from calling Kylie to see if she had got hold of Delphinia.

"No, not yet. I left her a message and told her it was urgent. I said you particularly wanted to talk to her. I said that after the warnings she had given you, it sent you into meltdown."

"Oh, well done. Let me know as soon as you've organised something." Dotty ended the call and felt a tap on the shoulder. It was her dad.

"I hope you're not getting mixed up in something you shouldn't be. I know what you're like for meddling."

"No, dad. Of course not. Would you like a cup of tea? I've got a couple of hours more work her and then I'll tidy up."

"Make sure you do and yes I will have a drink and in answer to your question, Delphinia had an alibi."

"What do you mean?"

"I overheard you talking. I'm not completely stupid and I know what's going on. The killings have been big news, so I spoke to my mate about how the investigation was going when we played golf this week. Delphina has someone to vouch for her whereabouts the night Fred was killed."

"Oh, I see."

"So, don't lie to your dad in future about what you're up to."

"No, I won't."

That was Dotty told. She had one batch of chocolates remaining to make when disaster struck. Somehow, through rushing to finish, the filling curdled, and she didn't have enough cream for the last batch anymore. The fruit and nut filling she planned to do was one of her best sellers. Her customers would lynch her if there wasn't enough for them. She took off her apron and sighed.

"Just nipping to the shop, Dad. Won't be long." Dotty usually walked to the High Street as it wasn't far, but on this occasion, she drove to save time. If her dad went into the kitchen while she was out, he was likely to have a coronary at the mess. She needed to rush back and get finished.

Dotty drove past The Old Six Bells where Kylie worked and as she slowed down to turn into Sainsbury's carpark, she noticed Royston stood outside the pub talking to someone. She couldn't make out who it was as she had to keep her eye on the traffic. Before entering the supermarket, she looked up and saw Royston was still there talking. Deciding to have a nosey, she wandered up towards the pub.

That was interesting. It was Winston, Delphinia's son. Dotty went over to speak to them. They didn't notice her approaching and were deep in conversation. Dotty caught the tail end of what they said.

"So, the ambush is still on for next Friday," Royston said. Winston was about to reply when he felt Dotty's presence and looked up.

"Hi, Winston, I've been trying to get hold of your mum." Winston looked at her as though she had grown an extra head. He didn't reply. Both young men stared at her. Winston rubbed the back of his neck and turned to Royston. His eyes narrowed. Dotty swallowed and tried to ignore the fact she had interrupted something. "Sorry, you probably don't remember me. I'm Dotty." She held out her hand to shake Winston's, but he kept his hands firmly in his pocket.

"She's that, alright." Royston laughed and nudged Winston. Dotty didn't take the bait and turned her body away from Royston.

"Your mum has done a couple of readings for me and I needed to see her about something she said. My friend left her a message, but Delphinia hasn't got back to us yet."

"So, what do you want me to do?" Winston sneered and shrugged his shoulders.

"If you wouldn't mind mentioning that you've seen me and ask her to ring either me or Kylie, that would be great."

He gave her a half-hearted nod. Dotty didn't think he would pass on any message. She couldn't wait to leave those two to their conniving. She turned on her heels and walked swiftly back to the shop.

Dotty was on pins to get home and phone Kylie and Rachel to tell them about the encounter with the boys. She was beaten to it by Rachel.

"We need to recruit Harry into our private investigator's ring. He's done a sterling job."

"Why? What's he uncovered now?"

"There's a lot goes on when you get into that dark web."

"I'm sure there is. What has he found out?"

"The White Brethren Society are planning a march this Friday. They're hoping to recruit more people to their cause. There will be a rally, followed by a meeting at Abingworth meadow. From what Harry read, they are keeping their views on their distaste for other cultures low-key and concentrating on discussing making Britain a greener place to live."

"Wait a minute, next Friday, you say?"

"Yes, that's right."

"I thought I heard Royston and Winston talking about an ambush next Friday. I don't know if I heard them right, but they could be linked."

"Do you think you ought to tell the police?"

"I'm not sure. What if I didn't hear correctly? I would look a fool."

"Maybe mention it to Dave then."

"Good idea. I haven't heard from him in a while. It would be a good excuse for me to get in touch."

Chapter 32

Dotty couldn't get hold of Dave, so she left a message saying there was something important she had to tell him. He replied that he also had something important to say to her. That sounded ominous. She wondered what it could be. He told her he was working until Sunday evening so asked if her news could wait until then. She decided that it could, so they arranged to meet up after her event finished.

Sunday morning, Dotty looked out the kitchen window as she got ready to pack her chocolates away. How things had changed in a few short weeks. Three weeks ago, snow had been forecast and this weekend, England was basking in a heatwave. That meant the barbecues were out in force and the area stunk of lighter fuel. Whilst Dotty loved to see the sun shining, her chocolates didn't. She would keep her fingers crossed that she was given a cool spot at the event.

The clear blue sky improved Dotty's mood and seeing that yellow ball in the sky was a bonus. It was a shame the nice weather was so sporadic. According to the weatherman, it was due to last for three days before the rain came back. It was the sort of day, for an outing to Brighton which was where Dotty would have preferred to be. This mini heatwave would do her sales no favours. No one bought chocolate in the sunshine.

She wheeled her truckload of goodies out to the car and wiped the perspiration off her brow. This wasn't a good sign, to be so warm so early. She prayed her confectionery would hold up in the heat. She arrived nice and early at the fair to get the best spot but as she walked into the large craft marquee, she groaned. It was like a greenhouse. She couldn't work in those conditions. Quickly, she went to find the organiser.

"Barbara, can I have a word, please." Barbara had just finished talking to a tall man and held a tight grip on her clipboard.

"Yes, what is it?" Barbara looked over her glasses.

"Is there anywhere else you can put me. The marquee is so hot, my chocolates will melt."

"Oh dear, not really. Let me think." A large woman with brown wavy hair walked up to speak to Barbara.

"I can't find my pitch. Are you sure you've numbered them correctly?"

"What was your name again?" Barbara asked the woman. Someone else came to have a word with her, hovering by her shoulder.

"What's wrong?" she asked.

"My electricity supply isn't working." Barbara looked at Dotty. "Give me a minute and I'll see what I can sort out for you."

Dotty felt downcast. She almost wished she hadn't come. Kylie wasn't joining her. After her confession about eating her products, Dotty now had to work alone so she wouldn't get a break unless she left her stall unmanned.

Dotty waited outside. Her skin already glistened from standing inside the tent. The sun beat down like the thermostat had broken. England didn't do air conditioning. There weren't enough hot days to warrant it, so when the heat came it was unbearable. Barbara hadn't even thought to bring along fans. Today would be like working in an inferno — sheer hell. Finally, Barbara came out to attend to Dotty.

"I understand your plight but there's not a lot I can do. The only thing I can suggest is, I have a small gazebo that I can put up over by the entrance area. You would have to work alone but at least it's in the shade."

"Okay, that will have to do." Dotty sighed. Half the fun of these events was chatting to other traders. Today she would have to sacrifice any networking for the sake of her chocolates' survival. People were already coming in, so she had to work quickly to set up her display. It was hot work. Sweat trickled down her back. Dotty's main priority was keeping her products in the shade. She hoped that would be enough to stop them from melting.

Everyone who walked past commented on the weather. The UK is probably the only place in the world where talking about the climate is the number one conversation topic. It takes up such a large portion of the day. That's mainly because every season can appear within a twenty-four-hour period and it can be so unpredictable. It wasn't unpredictable today though. This scorcher had been on the cards for a few days and people were getting prepared. Sun creams and designer sunglasses were out in force.

"What a lovely day."

"Too nice to be working in."

"We're getting our burgers and sausages in ready for tonight's barbecue."

Dotty listened to the comments of the people who wandered past her stall. She didn't want to be a killjoy and say she wasn't enjoying it. That was like sacrilege to say you weren't happy seeing the sunshine. She glanced down at her display. It was party time for the wasps who homed in on her chocolates. Dotty wafted them away.

Sales were slow which was as Dotty expected given how warm it was. She spent all her time fighting off the wasps and flies and keeping everything in the shade. She moved the trays around. Wearing her plastic see-through gloves, she tested to see how they were holding up. One or two batches were becoming dangerously soft.

"Hello, Dotty. I wondered if I'd see you here. How's the weather suiting you?"

"I'm struggling, Betty. If I'm not careful, this sun will melt everything."

"Oh, what a shame. All that work you put into making them will be wasted. I've just been talking to Lydia Farnham. She's doing a bomb selling her fruit smoothies."

"Good for her." Dotty could well do without Betty Simpson's comments.

"Oo, my back." Betty put a hand on her lower back.

"Are you okay, Betty? Do you want to sit down?" Dotty helped Betty to the chair behind her table. "Can I get you anything?"

"Pass me my handbag. I've got some painkillers in there. It's probably this heat that's making it worse." Dotty knew that if it were raining, Betty would blame that. In fact, whatever the weather was doing caused Betty's bad back to worsen according to her. As was the norm with Betty, she told Dotty all about her latest visit to the consultant, going over every word he said in detail. Dotty didn't like to stop her and say that Betty told her all this the previous week. She couldn't get a word in anyway. Finally, Betty took a breath but then immediately started up again.

"I hear that Christine Beckley was taken in for questioning over Nigel's death. They released her though. They don't think she did it."

Dotty nodded. Having Betty there wasn't all bad. At least she provided nuggets of information about the killings. You just had to listen to all the boring stuff first.

"Are those chocolates supposed to do that?" Betty pointed to one of the trays of truffles. Dotty had been so busy concentrating on Betty's yapping and her bad back, she took her mind off keeping her display out of the sun.

"Oh no!" It had only taken twenty minutes, but in that short space of time, tiny brown muddy puddles had appeared on half of the trays. The chocolates had turned to mush. What a disaster!

"I better leave you to it." Betty scarpered quickly leaving Dotty to clear up the mess. There was no point staying any longer. She packed up, threw ninety percent of the chocolate splodge away and sloped off home not sure if she still wanted to meet Dave later. Who knew that melted chocolate could put you in such a foul mood?

Chapter 33

Dotty still felt glum when she arrived to meet Dave that evening. She hoped his news wasn't something bad. The disaster with the chocolates had left a profound effect on her and she had spent the early evening evaluating her life. There were elements of her job she enjoyed but it was hard work for the returns she got. She couldn't see it as a long-term prospect. What she would give to have Mr Binns, the careers adviser from her schooldays here now telling her what to do. Do something creative, he had told her. Mm, what else could she put her mind to and make a success of?

She walked into the wine bar and glanced around the room. The nice weather had brought the crowds out and the bar was packed. The noise of chatter hummed through the air. Dave had already found a corner pew, and waved when he saw her. She shook her hand as if holding a glass to ask if he wanted anything. He declined so Dotty plumped for a large glass of Chablis. She took it over to where Dave sat and went up to him and kissed his cheek. He didn't respond. That brought a wave of discomfort to her stomach. His smile seemed forced. Something was wrong. She waited, but he didn't speak. She settled in the seat next to him and told him about the fiasco with the chocolates. He listened but looked distant as though he had something on his mind weighing him down.

"Is everything okay, Dave?"

"Yes, fine. What is it you wanted to talk to me about?" He avoided eye contact. He wasn't a very good liar. Dotty told him about eavesdropping on Royston and Winston's conversation and what she knew about the White Brethren Society and their impending gathering. Dave's face looked serious.

"You have been getting involved where you shouldn't, haven't you? What did I tell you not to meddle in police business?" Dave looked cross. Dotty felt like a naughty schoolgirl.

"I…" Dotty didn't know where to look or what to say. She had no excuses. "I… I thought the police would want to know."

"So, what else have you found out?" Dotty decided that if she had gone this far, she may as well tell him everything she knew. She told him about how she and her friends had done some investigation, specifically into Nigel's death to help her friend, Milly.

"Our suspects at first were Kylie's auntie Flo, Christine, Judith and Winston, Delphinia's son. They were all in the area and could have administered the poisonous mushrooms. Royston had also been added to the list as he had been to Millie's house and could possibly have found the batch of soup. We felt that he was the least likely to have done it because he wouldn't have known that Nigel would eat the mushroom soup. That put Christine as number one suspect as she talked him into trying some. Delphinia also wasn't too far away, and she was known to have a grudge against Nigel so, we haven't discounted her. In fact, all of them had cause to dislike him but was that enough to murder him?" After Dotty finished her speech, she waited. Dave didn't speak. He remained calm. Finally, he opened his mouth.

"I see." He nodded his head. "You have been very busy, and you lied to me."

"But I…" Dave put his hand up to stop Dotty speaking.

"You have got involved where you shouldn't." Dave took his phone out and made a call.

"Who are you phoning?" Dave ignored her but spoke into the phone.

"You better get over here, mate. I've something important to tell you."

Dave continued to ask Dotty questions about her involvement. His tone had changed to that of police officer. She didn't like it. He made her feel guilty when all she had been trying to do was to help a friend.

Ten minutes later, she groaned when she saw who walked through the door — Wayne.

"You need to hear this," Dave said to his colleague. Dotty relayed back everything she previously told Dave. Wayne listened. Finally, he turned to Dotty.

"So, Delphinia had been blackmailing Nigel and his cronies?"

"It appears that way from what we've found out." Wayne's face was serious.

"Okay, well I've got work to do." Wayne rose from the table they were sat around. "I'll deal with you later, young lady and I'll see you back at the nick, Dave."

Dotty wondered how much trouble she was in. If she didn't need a good strong drink before, she certainly needed one now.

"I'm sorry for lying to you. Fancy a cocktail as a peace offering?" She tried to get the mood back on track.

"Yeah, that's a good idea."

The drinks arrived and Dotty took a long glug of hers. Dave ordered a Malibu Beach and when he sipped through his straw, his head was obscured by the cherry, pineapple and umbrella. Dotty sidled up beside him. Her mind was ready to take off to some sun-kissed beach. She desperately wanted to imagine she was on holiday and get away from all this mess. Dotty was glad she had worn a summer dress. The heat was unbearable, even for early evening. Dave wore white shorts with a navy polo shirt. She glanced down at his legs feeling sure he must be wearing fake tan. His legs shone a golden colour. Not only that, but she was convinced he had shaved the hairs from them, his calves look moisturised and gleaming. Dotty resisted the urge to stroke them.

"You mentioned you had something important to tell me." After all the drama from her revelations, Dotty had almost forgotten about their previous conversation.

"Yes, that's right." Dave took a long swig of his drink then wiped around his mouth. He breathed in deeply then looked up to the ceiling. It looked as though he was praying under his breath.

"I've something I need to tell you."

"Yes." Dotty leaned forward.

"It's very difficult for me and I haven't told another soul about this yet."

"What is it, Dave?" Dotty's heart pounded but not half as much as Dave's. She hoped he wasn't going to say he didn't want to see her again as she enjoyed his company and thought they got on well.

"I… I've realised something after spending time with you."

"Yes?" Surely, he wasn't going to ask her to marry him.

"I enjoy your company and I love being with you."

"I feel the same, Dave," Dotty said, looking into his eyes. Dave glanced away.

"The thing is…"

"Yes."

"The thing is…" Dotty wanted to say — spit it out, but the way Dave was struggling with his words, she didn't want to appear insensitive.

"What is it, Dave? What are you trying to tell me?"

"Being with you has made me realise something very important." Dotty smiled. She felt sure now her hunch was right.

"And what is it you've realised?"

"That I'm gay." Dotty's mouth opened wide. Her eyes nearly popped out of her head. She didn't see that one coming. Her eyes moistened. That was not the news she expected.

"Oh, I see. What a brave thing to tell me. I hope that doesn't mean we can't still be friends?"

"No, of course not." Now, it all made sense to Dotty — why he never touched her or showed any intimacy towards her. It wasn't anything she had done wrong. She was disappointed and upset for herself. It had been a bad day all round. When she got home that night and had time to reflect, at least she felt pleased that she was the one who Dave came out to. Still, when it came to her love life, it was back to the drawing board.

Chapter 34

On Friday morning, Dotty sat in her kitchen watching the rain pelt down. Her mum and dad had gone away for the weekend for their wedding anniversary and her brother Joe was staying at his mate's, so she was home alone. That didn't help her mood any. In view of the disaster the previous week with her chocolates melting, she cancelled her event for that weekend as the weather was scheduled to be warm again. And it would have taken too much effort to put all the work in that was needed to produce enough stock. The whole affair had disheartened her.

Last Sunday had turned out to be a calamity. She hadn't heard from either Wayne or Dave since. Today was the day for the march scheduled by the White Brethren Society. She would keep well out of things. What happened had nothing to do with her. After telling the police what she and her friends had uncovered about the blackmailing, she wondered if Delphinia had been arrested yet. It was obvious now why she had been so against Dotty getting involved and warning her, it was because she was responsible.

Dotty made herself a drink and sat at the kitchen table thinking things over. Life never turned out the way you expected it to. As much as she wanted to keep out of things, she couldn't help herself. It was like she had two parrots sat on her shoulder. The well-behaved one saying, do as you're told and don't meddle in things that have nothing to do with you and the naughty parrot, on the other shoulder who said, aren't you curious to know who killed Nigel and Fred. It was the naughty parrot that got the better of her. On a hunch, she phoned Delphinia. She wanted to know if she was in police custody. The fortune teller still hadn't got back to her after the previous messages she left.

Dotty was surprised when Delphinia answered.

"I wondered if we could meet up?" Dotty asked.

"I could come over to you. I'll be there in two hours."

"Okay."

Was it a good idea to see Delphinia on her own? Probably not but she planned to tell her she thought Christine was responsible for the killings. She told Kylie what she was doing. Neither Kylie nor Rachel could be there due to work commitments. She'd have preferred some support in challenging Delphinia.

Dotty pottered around the house while she waited. She hoovered the bedrooms to gain some brownie points for when her parents came home. She even decided to place some fresh flowers in her mum and dad's room for their return. With no money to buy any, there were enough blooms in the garden to put together a nice bunch. Nipping in the shed for the secateurs, she weaved around the plants, snipping off a selection that had flowered to gain a varied selection. Then she mixed the daffodils with the lilies, tulips and a sprig of freesias. Since attending the flower arranging course, Dotty now took more care getting the design right rather than lobbing them all together. She did one display for the lounge and another for her parents' bedroom. Winnie had stayed at her side all the while she walked around the garden and had followed her back into the house not wanting to be left out. The dog watched as she snipped off the ends of the stalks and painstakingly arranged the various colours of pink, white, lilac and purple.

"There, Winnie. They look nice, don't they?" She breathed in the scent from the display. Pleased with her work, Dotty checked her watch for the time. Delphinia shouldn't be long now. She quickly fed Winnie while she waited. Then she remembered to put the secateurs back. She would just have time to return them to the shelf where they were always stored in the shed. There was no way she would leave them out and be on the receiving end of her dad's wrath. He was a stickler for everything being in its place.

She opened the front door and walked towards the shed at the back of the house. Unlocking the shed door, she was about to step inside. She hadn't heard the car pull up outside, but she did hear footsteps behind her. An arm went on her shoulder and she swivelled around.

"Delphinia, you made me jump."

Delphinia's face looked serious.

"Winston tells me you overheard his plans for the march later today."

"I…"

"Have you told the police what you heard?"

"No," Dotty lied.

"Good."

Next thing, an arm grabbed hold of Dotty's torso and pushed her into the shed. Up against the larger woman's frame, Dotty didn't stand a chance. She was overpowered and stumbled to the floor. By the time she recovered her stance and went to pick herself up, she heard the lock rumble.

"Hey!" she called out. She frowned and turned around to face the door. She put a thumb on the latch to open it, but nothing happened. She tried again. The door didn't budge. Pushing her weight against the wooden frame, she gave it a heave, but the door was fast shut. She rattled the latch but to no avail.

Her heart pounded as she realised what had happened. Delphinia had locked her in.

"Hey," she called out again but Delphinia didn't answer. So much for getting her over to question her about what she knew. Dotty stamped her feet, annoyed with herself for letting her guard down. She had been outsmarted. She sighed. Unfortunately, she didn't even have her phone with her. She had left it in the house. Delphinia's actions had convinced her she was behind the killings, but there was little she could do about it in this confined space. She looked around for something to help her escape.

The shed was her dad's pride and joy. Empty terracotta pots lined up along one shelf. There were some tiny seedlings in pots of soil on the table coming into bud. Worried about what her dad would do if she damaged the door, Dotty dismissed the idea of breaking it down. She would bide her time. Taking out a small watering can, she watered the plants. This gave her a thinking period. Occasionally, she called out.

"Is anybody there? Let me out." Her cries were wasted. There was no one outside to reply. More time passed.

Suddenly, she heard scraping at the door.

"Winnie, is that you?" Dotty heard a bark and smiled. "Get help, Winnie. There's a good dog."

Chapter 35

In the meantime, there had been developments across the road.

It was rare for Kylie's auntie Flo to come visiting in the neighbourhood, but it was an unusual request she received from Betty Simpson. She had bumped into her on the High Street the previous week. Flo told her about her revolutionary cure for pain relief, so Betty decided she wanted to try this wonder drug. Flo couldn't imagine Betty smoking a joint so instead agreed to bring over some of her cake.

Betty twitched the curtains in her front lounge as she spotted the car pull up outside Dotty's house.

"Is everything okay, Betty?" Flo asked as she cut them both a large slab of cake.

"Yes, I just wondered who is visiting the Drinkwater's place." Her head bobbed up and down and she squinted to see who it was. "It's that Delphinia and her son. What on earth are they doing? They were round the back of the house and now they're heading towards their car. Hang on a minute, Flo. I'll be with you in a jiffy." Betty scurried out of the house.

Flo had already had a few bites of the cake. Betty could do whatever she wanted. She returned within minutes and brought in a couple of guests.

"Is there enough cake for Delphinia and Winston to try?"

"Yes, there's enough here for everyone." Winston had the march that afternoon on his mind but the pull of getting stoned on space cake was preferable to attending any rally right now. Winston and Delphinia eagerly dived into a slice of cake.

"Mm, this is delicious, Flo." Delphinia licked her lips. Her head soon became fuzzy.

The women chatted away and Winston sat in the corner on his own watching the fish in the tank. He tried to copy the fishes' movements. It looked most strange. His mouth opened and shut in time with the fish and he flapped his body as though treading water then began to giggle. The women ignored him.

"Did you call to see Dotty?"

"Err, yes, Winston rang the doorbell while I was on the phone. She wasn't in." Delphinia's eyes centred on a vase on the table.

"Was that why I saw you round the back of the house?" Delphinia wriggled in the chair, still looking at the ceramic vase.

"Yes, that's right."

"We should ask Delphinia to do a reading for us and tell our future, Flo." Betty nudged Flo who looked up at the ceiling.

"Mm, good idea. Isn't your wallpaper a pretty colour?"

"Why thank you. I believe this stuff is working. My back feels much better."

"I told you it was good."

"It has made me feel a little strange though. I'm sure I can hear barking."

"No, you must be imagining things," Delphinia said.

Betty cocked her head to one side and frowned.

"Ssh, everybody." She could definitely hear a dog and it sounded close by. She rose from the chair to investigate. Flo and Delphinia didn't even notice her leave the room. They were busy talking about reggae music. It had surprised Delphinia to find someone with the same taste in music as her. Even Winston joined in the conversation about Desmond Dekker and Steel Pulse with Flo.

"Bob Marley is the greatest, but I also like Jimmy Cliff and Toots," Flo felt giddy. She had a captive audience and together they discussed their favourite sounds.

"Yeah man, we're kicking up rumpus here." Delphina shook her plaited hair. "Lordie, Lordie, I do declare, this woman knows her stuff." She high-fived Flo who giggled away. Flo took her phone out and scrolled down to select some music.

"*Whaat!* You got some of Shaggy's sounds? Atta girl. Put it on." Delphina encouraged Flo to turn the volume up to listen to the track.

Betty went into the kitchen to listen if she could hear where the noise was coming from. There was a scratching sound at her back door. She opened it and looked down to see Winnie. The poor little dog looked distressed. She wouldn't keep still. She grabbed hold of Betty's skirt and tried to pull her out.

"Whatever's got into you, Winnie? What's the matter?" The dog kept looking over at her own house. "Has Dotty locked you out? That's not like your owner, is it? She's normally very good with you. You can come in if you want but you must behave." But the little poodle had no intention of going into Betty's house. She stood there looking up at Betty and barking. "Pack it in, Winnie. There's no need to get yourself in a flap like this. If you're not coming in, I'll have to shut the door on you." Betty went to close the door, but Winnie pushed inside, and the yapping grew louder.

"Oh, Winnie. How does Dotty put up with all this noise? Do you want something to eat, is that it? Here let me see what I've got. Dogs don't eat chocolate, do they?" Betty rummaged through her kitchen larder. Winnie continued to bark. Betty put her hands over her ears. "Come on, Winnie. Stop barking. You're not usually like this when Dotty leaves you." Suddenly, a thought struck her. "Is Dotty okay? Is that what all this barking is about? Have you come to tell me something? Come on, Winnie. Let's go over and have a look."

As soon as Betty walked up the path towards Dotty's house, she heard the shouting coming from the shed.

"Dotty, is that you in there?"

"Yes, Betty, I've been locked in." Betty glanced down at the padlock but there was no key. She shouted out to tell Dotty. "There's a spare under the large stone next to the garage door." Betty went to retrieve the key and soon had Dotty out.

"What's going on?" She frowned looking at a flustered Dotty.

"That's what I'd like to know. Delphina locked me in." Betty looked across at her own house and frowned. "What? What is it, Betty?"

"Delphinia and Winston are in my house with Flo eating space cake."

"She was supposed to be coming here. Listen, phone the police and don't go back to your house. I don't think it's safe. Somehow, we need to get Flo out of there. I believe it was Delphinia who murdered Nigel and Fred. Her son is planning to ambush the White Brethren Society march this afternoon. I was locked in the shed to stop me from saying anything. Delphinia blackmailed their organisation probably because of racist comments or actions."

"I'm shocked. That's incredible. How can we get Flo out?"

"That woman is dangerous, and Flo could be in real trouble. Stay here, Betty. I'm going in."

It was walking up Betty's path that a thought came to Dotty. Something wasn't right. A memory that she had forgotten about came back to her. She had been a fool. The truth had been staring her in the face.

Delphinia, Flo and Winston didn't hear Dotty walk into Betty's house. She stood in the doorway and called Flo.

"Flo, can I have a word, please." Dotty signalled for Flo to come to the door, but Flo was having none of it. She patted the sofa.

"No, come and join us, Dotty. We're having a tea party, aren't we, guys?"

"Please, Flo. It's important I speak to you."

Delphinia and Winston picked up on Dotty's nervousness. They wanted to ask how she had got out of the shed, but they couldn't say anything without giving the game away.

"Flo wants to stay here, don't you, Flo?" Winston grabbed Flo around the neck.

"Easy, tiger." Flo wasn't happy about how Winston manhandled her, but he didn't let go of his grip. It was only when he pulled out a knife that Dotty and Flo gasped. He held it to Flo's throat.

"Winston, don't do anything stupid. Betty has called the police and they are on the way. The game's up. I know it was you who killed Nigel and Fred."

"What makes you say that?" Delphinia asked.

"Have you ever heard of an organisation called Stargazer's?" Dotty asked. Delphinia shook her head.

"No, I didn't think so, but Winston knows all about it, don't you, Winston?" He didn't reply but kept the knife at Flo's throat.

"Your son blackmailed The White Brethren Society. At first, I thought it was all your doing but then something struck me. What was the reason for blackmailing the organisation? Was it the racist remarks they said?"

"Nigel hired him to do some work on his house and when he found out Winston was black; he wouldn't let him in. He said some scathing things about our race," Delphinia replied. "He and his friends treated us like scum. If Winston blackmailed them, they only got what they deserved. We know our rights under the Race Discrimination laws. Good for him for not letting them get away with it."

"Yes, but they stopped paying you didn't they Winston, so you took revenge. I know how they behaved towards you wasn't right, but it's no reason to kill someone."

"You know nothing, you're all the same, you're white middle-class trash."

"Enough," came a voice behind Dotty. "I'll take over here." Dotty turned around to see DS Collins walk in with Wayne. "Hand over the knife, Winston. We don't want anyone else to get hurt."

Chapter 36

"How did you figure out it was Winston, Dotty? Kylie asked at weekend, as they sat in the café eating cream doughnuts.

"It was simple. He was the one who came along and said there was a fly in his soup."

"I don't get it. How does that make him a murderer?"

"Because he wanted Nigel dead, but he didn't want to kill the whole of Billingshurst or whoever else had the soup."

"But how did he know that Nigel would ask for mushroom soup?"

"Easy, he found out that Nigel was a vegetarian, and the mushroom was the only soup that Millie had on that didn't have meat in it. It could have all gone wrong of course. He may have had to resort to the tactics he did with Fred, calling him to a secret location to discuss the fact his payments had stopped. He just got lucky with Nigel, or unlucky if you look at it from Nigel's point of view."

"And was Delphinia in on all of this?"

"She knew about the White Brethren Society, but I don't think she had any idea her son was blackmailing them. He must have forged her signature to set up the account. I doubt she suspected he was the killer."

"Huh, and she calls herself a fortune teller!"

"I heard that the march went ahead as planned," Rachel said.

"Yes, they weren't ambushed. Without Winston there to lead them, the rival group didn't have the same clout." Dotty raised her eyebrows.

"The good thing is, because of the murders, the national press picked up on the White Brethren Society. There has been an outcry amongst the locals. The organisation has had to disband." Kylie sipped her coffee.

"Yes, the villagers have been up in arms." Dotty poured out a refill.

"I can't imagine Julian Cranston, the lawyer getting much work now he has been ousted because of his extreme views. It will affect his business for sure," Rachel said.

"I hear Judith Hastings has put her house up for sale." Kylie took another drink.

"It's probably for the best. Nigel left her with debts. It'll be interesting to see if Christine and Edna can still work together after everything that's gone on." Dotty looked across at her friends.

"I heard they're going to bring in two extra judges for future fairs. That should be interesting. To think we thought Christine was the murderer, all because she knew her mushrooms." Kylie raised her eyebrows.

"Well, we can't get everything right. Talking of which, I have some news."

"What's that then?" Rachel asked.

"I'm going to give up my chocolate business. I've enrolled for a college course."

"What are you going to do, criminology?" Kylie asked.

"No, I'll leave detective work to the police in future. I've decided to become a hairdresser and beauty therapist."

"Wow, good for you. I think you'll do well at that."

"I agree. Great idea, but somehow I can't see you keeping your nose out if there are any more killings in the area." Kylie bit into the new recipe citrus Eccles cake.

"No, trust me. I won't get involved."

"If you hadn't acted so promptly, Kylie's auntie Flo might no longer be with us."

"Yes, thanks for that, Dotty."

"I know, she appreciated my involvement and sent me some flowers."

"It's just a shame the police didn't appreciate your input as well."

"No, I've made a lifelong enemy in Wayne."

"He'll be jealous of the glory you and Winnie have been getting."

"Yes, and talking of Winnie, I bought her a big bag of treats as a reward for getting me out of the shed."

"Well, we're proud of you. Winston will go to prison for a long time thanks to you."

"Don't you mean, thanks to us? It helped that he had the same knife on him that he went to threaten Flo with that he previously used on Fred."

"I still don't believe the police would have cracked this without you."

"We were a team, you two, Harry, and even Betty helped and of course, how could I forget Winnie."

"No, good old Winnie. Your dog is a legend!"

Dotty Dreads a Disaster is Book 2 in the Dotty Drinkwater Mystery series.

I hope you enjoyed it.

All my books can be read as standalones but they do run in sequence so if you want to be there at the start, you can follow the progress of the main protagonist.

I am looking to build a relationship up with my readers, so I send out FREE books in my newsletters for people who join my VIP club. The weekly bulletins include otherwise untold information about the characters, things about me, and other bits of news including freebies and offers.

I would love you to join and in return for giving me your email which will never be passed on to third parties, you will receive exciting goodies and give-aways not found anywhere else.

You can find the sign-up page on my website at:

http://dezzardwriter.com/mc4wp-form-preview

Website: http://dezzardwriter.com/
Email: support@dezzardwriter.com
Facebook:
https://www.facebook.com/dezzardwriter/
Twitter: https://twitter.com/diane_ezzard

REVIEWS

If you enjoyed this book, I would greatly appreciate if you would leave a review.
Just a few short words on Amazon and maybe Goodreads and Bookbub would go a long way towards helping me.
Your encouragement helps stoke the fires of my creativity.

To improve my writing and to spur me on to write more, it is important that I get feedback from you, my readers.
Your opinion matters to me.
I greatly appreciate your time and effort.

You can click on the link below to leave a review, thankyou.

mybook.to/dottydis

ABOUT THE AUTHOR

Manchester born Diane Ezzard writes emotionally charged mystery books about ordinary people dealing with everyday situations until something goes badly wrong. (There is usually a dead body in there somewhere).

Her first series - the Sophie Brown Mystery Series is dark and gritty. The second series - the Dotty Drinkwater Mystery Series is a cozy, full of zany lighthearted escapades.

In a previous life, she worked as a HR manager, counsellor and managed a charity among many other jobs where she has picked up a lot of her material from.

She now lives and works in South-East England close to her daughter and young grandchildren where she spends her time fighting pirates and dinosaurs when not writing.

ACKNOWLEDEMENTS

I would like to give a big thank you to Samantha Ezzard for another great looking cover.

I would also like to give a special mention to Gracie Kennedy for her help in plot development. I don't know where I would have been without her wacky sense of humour and her ability to help me think out of the box. Her enthusiasm really spurred me on.

Thanks go especially to my team of readers, ARC group and my fan base. Without your praise and encouragement, I would not be as motivated to write.

LINKS: -

Website: http://dezzardwriter.com/
Email: support@dezzardwriter.com
Facebook: https://www.facebook.com/dezzardwriter/
Twitter: https://twitter.com/diane_ezzard
Bookbub: http://bit.ly/2OlnLE1
Amazon: https://amzn.to/2Qf2uZV

Dotty Dices with Death
Book 1 in the Dotty Drinkwater Mystery Series.

"Suspicious death of local DJ," read the headlines. The man of Dotty's dreams turns into something of a nightmare.

Meeting the tall, dark, handsome foreigner at her new job in the casino, Dotty thought all her Christmases had come at once. Instead, she discovers a trail of lies and deceit, to say nothing of a suspicious package. Was Dotty the last one to see him alive? Do the police suspect she is involved?

With the help of her friends, Dotty sets out to unravel the mystery around the tragic murder before she gets locked up herself. She should never have ignored the warning given by the mystery woman.

Chapter 1

Dotty took off her fluffy olive-green beanie hat and scratched the top of her head. She made her way to the back of the bus and found an empty seat by the window. As CEO of her own company, it wasn't ideal travelling this way. It couldn't be helped, however, as her car had been making that funny noise again. She wouldn't put up with it any longer. After all, it might be something serious and she could hardly run her gardening business with no vehicle. So, she dropped it off at the garage first thing. It was handy that she had no customers booked in today other than a potential new client to visit. She'd look strange getting on the bus with a lawnmower and other gardening tools. What would her nosey neighbour, Betty Simpson think? There would be no end of moaning from Betty if she took up extra room with her equipment. Nudging Betty who sat on the seat in front, she smiled.

"Cold out, today," she said.

"Yes, dear. Where's your car?" Betty didn't miss a trick. She was the go-to person if you wanted to hear any gossip.

"It's in the garage for a service." That wasn't the whole truth but sometimes a little white lie was the easiest option with Betty. Dotty was in no mood for explaining irregular car noises this morning. Betty didn't need to know the ins and outs. She embroidered stories enough and came up with her own version, anyway. Knowing Betty, if she decided that Dotty's car had really been towed away for getting behind with the repayments, then that's what she would tell everyone. Betty could tarnish your name with her misrepresentations before you could click your fingers.

Dotty thought about changing her car for a van. It would be more practical, but it didn't go with her image and street cred. Besides, she was fed up of gardening. It was okay in the summer months when the weather was warmer but now the colder weather had set in, there wasn't as much to do, and it was freezing working outside. She'd not given that much thought when she was talked into starting up this little one-woman business by her two friends, Rachel and Kylie.

It was alright for them. They both had their nice warm jobs working inside. Rachel worked in an office and Kylie worked as a barmaid at Ye Olde Six Bells. Neither girl was happy in their jobs, but they weren't as miserable as Dotty. They always had a moan when the threesome met up on a Saturday. Although, if they all wanted to go on holiday together next year, they would have to grin and bear it.

Dotty wasn't on the bus for long. She checked the address beforehand and knew which stop to get off. If the Braithwaite's hadn't lived at the top of a hill, she'd have taken her pushbike, but it was too steep to tackle, and the forecast was for rain later. She shuddered and vowed to put some effort into looking for a new job. There had to be better ways than this to make a living. It could be worse. She could be in India working in the paddy fields or — no she couldn't think of any jobs worse than gardening right now. Even India would be warmer than Sussex. She looked out the window and watched a gust of wind pick up the leaves as they took flight through the air.

Dotty arrived at the location and jumped off the bus. She immediately felt the chill of the wind on her cheeks. She tossed her head back and walked up to the house. Her mind wandered as she thought about working in a bar in Ibiza or picking strawberries in Portugal, anything warm away from this biting cold weather. She looked up at the large house and groaned as she rang the doorbell. The door creaked open and the tall, pinched face of Mr Braithwaite stared down at her as she stood waiting on the bottom step.

"Oh, you're a girl. Well, I suppose its women's lib, and anything goes these days. You'd better come through." He walked in front and Dotty scurried behind. "It's a girl, Marjorie. It's a girl." Dotty thought it sounded like someone had just given birth.

"Yes, I know it is, Albert. Now run along and make yourself useful." Albert stood in the doorway frowning. "Make a drink." She shooed him out of the room. "Have a seat. Dotty, isn't it?"

Dotty nodded and plonked herself down on a grey corduroy sofa. The Braithwaite couple were retired, and Mrs Braithwaite had seen Dotty's card in the local hairdresser's shop. Albert returned not long after with a tray of drinks and a plate of chocolate digestives. Under normal circumstances, Dotty would refuse the biscuits as she was dieting again, but she took one to be polite.

"Take a few. We only get them in for guests. We both have diabetes and can't eat them." Dotty thought it strange to buy biscuits they couldn't eat, so she took another two to show her consideration and smiled. She finished her drink and Marjorie asked her all the questions she could think of. Marjorie wanted to know more about Dotty's family than finding out her prowess as a gardener. In fact, the only question relating to gardening was about her age.

"You look very young to have your own gardening business, dear."

"I'm twenty-seven."

"Gosh, you don't look that old." Dotty believed her youthful looks were more down to her beauty regime than her genes. She used a face pack twice a week, exfoliated on alternate days, always used serum and moisturiser and gave her face a deep cleanse every bedtime. She had also recently splashed out on eye cream and neck cream because you can't be too careful. Wrinkles could appear any time. With all the effort she put in, she hoped to still look youthful in her sixties and seventies if she could keep up her efforts until then.

"Thank you," Dotty said, blushing.

"So, you're not married, yet?" Marjorie asked as she pointed to Dotty's bare wedding ring finger.

"No, I'm very much single. My last relationship was a disaster. Ray was a nightmare to get rid of. He just wouldn't take no for an answer. We were only together for a short time and it's taken me months to get him to see I'm not interested."

"Oh dear, young love never runs smooth. Those were the days. I knew straightaway when I met my Albert that he was the one for me. You know immediately, don't you, dear?"

"I wish Ray could have worked out sooner he wasn't the one for me. He must have been thick not to get the message." Marjorie gave a shallow sigh. From her nostalgic gaze, she was no longer listening to Dotty. Her memory cells sprang forward with visions of Albert as a young man with his long hair. They were both teenagers in the Swinging Sixties but were more mod than rocker. Albert owned a gleaming blue scooter and would take Marjorie on day trips to Southend. Ah, those were the days.

"Would you like me to show you the work we want you to do?" Marjorie asked, coming back into the moment.

"Yes, of course."

"Follow me. There's a lot." Marjorie pulled a face. "Albert can't do it anymore with his bad back."

They walked around to the back of the house. Dotty was taken out to the garden.

"Wow, that's huge."

"Yes, it's rather deceptive. You can't tell from the front of the house just how much land is round the back. As you can see, we have a lot of trees which means a lot of leaves." Dotty had never seen as many leaves as those sat in the Braithwaites' garden. It was as though they had been collecting them up for her. "Do you have one of those machines that hoover them up?"

"No, but I'm sure I can get hold of one." She stood admiring the hues of orange and brown that nature produced in autumn just before the harshness of winter took the last few leaves away. There were speckles of yellow and red to inspire her creative juices. As Dotty spoke, a gust of wind brought another ton of leaves swirling into the garden. She worried that as soon as one set of leaves cleared, another would appear. She'd have preferred to be out there painting the scenery rather than clearing it away.

The two women stood together viewing the spectacle for some time. More leaves fell from the interlocking branches of the trees above. This would be a thankless task. It wasn't a good idea to take this job on, but Dotty needed the money. She was at the stage of borrowing off her mum to go on a night out and that wasn't good.

They moved into the kitchen to discuss terms. Dotty didn't know how much hiring a leaf machine would set her back, so she added on extra to compensate. She showed Marjorie the price as she seemed to be in charge and the one holding the purse strings in this house. They had just shaken on the deal when a crashing sound came from the hall. Both women looked at each other with raised eyebrows.

"It's only me, Gran," came a voice that Dotty thought she recognised. She frowned and seconds later a tall young man stood at the kitchen door.

"Oh, it's you. What are you doing here?" he swept his lanky fringe off to the side.

"Hello, Ray. How are you?" Dotty had a sickly feeling growing inside her stomach.

"Do you two know each other?" Marjorie looked at them both.

Book One in the Sophie Brown series –

I KNOW YOUR EVERY MOVE

A sinister phone call, an unknown visitor. Sophie's life is about to be turned upside down

Sophie has worked hard to free herself from the clutches of addiction and turn her life around. Practising as a counsellor, in a women's centre in Manchester, she now helps other girls in trouble.
She forms a close relationship with Cassie, one of her clients and tries to help her escape the clutches of a violent boyfriend.
But is Sophie being followed?
How can she uncover the truth, when she can't trust what is real?
The more she delves, the closer she gets to danger.

Can she revisit her own dark past before it is too late?
Get hooked on this dark, twist-filled suspense thriller that's in the vein of works by Rachel Abbott and Mark Edwards.

Chapter One

YESTERDAY

Something soft and feathery brushed past the end of my nose. I sneezed and opened my eyes.

"Oh Max," I said.

The vision of loveliness that met me made me smile. What an adorable furry sight to wake up to in the morning. Sat on top of the silver satin duvet cover lay Max, the new addition to my family. At twelve-weeks-old, Max was a cute, mischievous bundle of joy. With big doleful eyes looking up at me, my heart melted. I stroked his velvety golden coat and tickled him under his chin.

"Want your breakfast, Max?"

I ignored the sound of him purring as I pressed my phone and looked at the time. 6.42. I groaned. I didn't need to get up early today. It was Saturday, so no work and I'd had a fitful night's sleep.

I'd had that dream again. The same one I'd been having over the last few months. I was running away from something or someone. I didn't know what, but I always woke up full of tension and fear. Thankfully, I never got caught. One minute I was jogging by the river, on my usual route, the next I'd been transported to a house. The combination of the red poppy wallpaper and mint green leather sofa was a scene I knew well from my childhood. Mum stood by the mirror in the hall, carefully putting on her lipstick. She wore the last outfit I'd seen her in, a tan polo neck ribbed jumper and fawn herringbone tweed skirt. I pulled at her arm.

"Please come, Mum." She didn't acknowledge me.

"Mum, come on, we need to go." No response.

"Hurry up Mum." Still, she ignored me.

I wasn't happy. Whether it was the bright shade of her crimson lip colour I didn't like or the fact she didn't respond to me, I didn't know.

In the dream, I began to panic as I sensed trouble brewing. I kept looking around. I had to act now. I tried one last time, shaking her.

"Mum, Mum, we've got to leave." She continued to face the mirror.

"Come on Mum, we've got to go."

I shouted out, but Mum still didn't acknowledge me. I began to cry. Fear enveloped me. I knew we were in danger. I watched her as she slowly applied another coat of lipstick and massaged her lips against each other. She didn't respond to me, so I turned away from her and ran.

That was when I woke up. Slowly, I re-entered the land of the living with a big stretch. Max jumped off the bed. My palms were sweating, and my pulse was racing. The anxiety rose in my chest. I had left Mum again and even though I knew it was only a dream, I didn't feel good. My stomach ached as I thought of the memories of her.

Might as well get up now I'm awake, I thought and walked over to open the curtains. I squinted as I looked outside. It wasn't the brightness of the day that greeted me. The clouds looked grey and forlorn. I begrudgingly put my dressing gown on and pottered into the kitchen.

I had Max now to look after, and I enjoyed spoiling him. My first job in a morning was to get him a saucer of milk and his food.

"Come on Max, here's your breakfast," I said. He didn't even give me the chance to get the food out of the can. He had his nose busy poking inside, trying to get at the fishy delights.

There weren't many places for a kitten to wander around and explore, especially with a flat as small as mine. When he got bigger, I knew I would have to let him out to discover the big wide world, and that scared me.

After feeding Max, I reached up into the cupboard to get the breakfast cereal. I sat for a few minutes, crunching a mouthful of fruit and fibre, contemplating the day ahead. Saturday usually meant doing chores which I detested, followed by a trip down to the shops to get my groceries for the weekend.

Shopping list done, I began milling around the place, starting with tidying up the kitchen. After walking into the hall to get the mop out of the cupboard, I checked myself out in the mirror.

My hair looked tangled, so I picked up the hairbrush and brushed it. It had a sheen and style that many women envied. I loved the comments I got about my beautiful long red locks.

The flat never seemed lonely on a Saturday, thanks to James Martin. Saturday Morning Kitchen was a favourite TV programme of mine. It formed part of my weekend ritual that included eating a bacon butty for lunch and a curry later that night. I didn't think of myself as a creature of habit, but there were certain behaviours that ran so deep, they were a regular part of my life now.

I had a passion for food, which spanned from cooking to watching cookery programmes on TV. I owned a vast range of recipe books and of course, I loved eating. Thankfully, I enjoyed running, as my frame would have been a lot larger had I not.

I wasn't one to try new recipes; I usually kept to classics like chilli and fish pie. I often dreamed of being the head chef of a Michelin-starred restaurant. Sadly, the culinary skills I possessed fell a long way short of that. Sometimes, I'd be in the shower, merrily singing away and realise that the sound accompanying me wasn't violins but the smoke detector going off in the other room. I would then remember that I'd put a couple of rashers of bacon under the grill.

I was concentrating on watching Rick Stein making a fish stew before getting up to tackle the ironing. Wrestling to put the ironing board up wasn't easy in the small confines of the kitchen. There was very little room to manoeuvre. I sighed heavily and frowned. I didn't like housework, least of all the ironing.

Suddenly the house phone rang. The old-fashioned cream coloured telephone sat a few feet from where I stood. I'd bought it to tone in with my muted decor. The penetrating sound of the intermittent bell ringing made me jump, and with jerked shoulders, I listened intently to the shrill tone. It was unusual to hear the house phone these days. Most people phoned me on my mobile. In fact, I only used the landline for the internet, so I couldn't imagine who it could be. Only Dad rang me on the landline, and we had a set time every Sunday night to speak. He never detracted from that, so I knew it couldn't be him. I decided not to answer. It was probably one of those PPI compensation calls or the ones that ask if you've been involved in an accident.

The phone got louder with every ring. The noise had distracted me from the ironing, and lacking concentration, I hadn't realised that I'd misjudged the iron plate. The hot iron toppled over, and I instinctively put my hand out to catch it.

Damn, I swore under my breath. The heat of the iron burnt through to my fingers and I screamed out. I was annoyed with myself for being so stupid. I quickly managed to shimmy past the ironing board to get to the sink. I put my hand under the cold-water tap. Ow, did that hurt. I kept my fingers under the icy blast of water, and I heard the phone still ringing.

That didn't sound like a friendly bell, more like the harsh warning sound of a siren. The loud noise blocked out the pleasant familiar tones of the omelette competition on TV. I urged the phone to stop. My heart pounded, and my fingers throbbed with pain. Why didn't it stop? I became irritated. The constant sound of the phone began to take on a macabre tone, and I became afraid to remove my hand from under the cold flow of water. Should I answer? No, I've left it this long.

My mind started playing tricks on me. Memories flooded back of a time when I had been trapped in the clutches of someone else's obsessions. A shudder came over me. What if it's him? No, I knew I was being silly now.

What if it's important? Pull yourself together, girl. If it's urgent, they'll leave a message, I told myself. I turned the tap off at the same time the phone stopped ringing. I picked up the remote control and turned off the TV.

The silence was eerie, and I could feel the thudding of my pulse. A knot churned over in my stomach and nausea crept up from my guts into my throat. My palms started to sweat, and the perspiration dripped from my forehead. My mouth was dry. A tightness developed in my chest and I bit my lip. Why was I getting so nervous about a phone ringing?

I walked over to the table, tentatively picking up the receiver with my good hand. My nerves erupted when I heard the tone that indicated there had been a message left. Stop getting so worked up, girl.

This was stupid. Breathing rapidly, I took the phone to my ear. A wave of cold air came over me as I listened intently. And I listened, and I listened. Nothing. I breathed a sigh of relief. Probably one of those nuisance companies, I thought.

I shook my throbbing hand and decided to leave the ironing until another time. I went into the bathroom to get a shower. I stood under the hot water for longer than normal and I chastised myself for getting so worked up over the phone. The water poured down, covering my body. The heat of it felt good. My fingers were still smarting. The shower door normally gave adequate sound proofing but, even with soap in my ears, I heard the ringtone of the house phone again.

I'll leave it, I thought to myself. It's probably the same annoying company that rung earlier. The ringing had stopped by the time I got out but, when I reached for the towel, it started up again. I was becoming irritated now.

Briskly drying myself down, I put on my dressing gown then went back into the kitchen to make myself a drink. I put the water in the kettle. The phone started ringing again. Whoever was phoning certainly wasn't taking no for an answer, so I decided to check the phone for messages in case an emergency had come up.

I knew I shouldn't be agitated over this, but I'd had such bad experiences in the past with menacing calls. I now had an unfounded fear around phones. Blind panic overwhelmed me as I listened and heard the distorted robot-like voice of a text call coming through the receiver.

"DON'T THINK YOU CAN GET AWAY WITH THIS."

What on earth did that mean? Get away with what? It was a strange message, and I didn't understand. Then I realised there was another message to listen to, so I pressed the button and waited.

In the same spooky, tinny voice of technology I heard, "SLUTS END UP GETTING WHAT THEY DESERVE." I started shaking.

I wondered if I could have misheard the messages so played them again. No, there was no mistaking the words. I pressed in the digits to find out the number the calls had been sent from, but the voice came back, 'Caller number withheld.'

I walked over to the sofa and sat down, my shoulders hunched, slowly taking in what had just happened. I wrapped my arms around my body and rocked from side to side, thinking. Was this a wrong number and all a mistake or could this be something more sinister?

Bibliography

The Sophie Brown Mystery Series –

My Dark Decline – prequel

One woman's journey from oblivion to recovery

I Know Your Every Move – Book 1

A sinister phone call, an unknown visitor — is Sophie being followed?

As Sick As Our Secrets - Book 2

Secrets and lies are rife in the dark world of gangsters and criminals.

The Sinister Gathering - Book 3

Sophie went on a retreat hoping to find peace, instead, she found the body of a woman she had just met

Resentments and Revenge – Book 4

A murdered young woman, a missing schoolboy, are they connected?

A Life Lost – Book 5

She lost her memory and then her life.

The Killing Cult – Book 6

Sophie makes a horrific discovery when she stumbles on a deadly cult.

The Dotty Drinkwater Mystery Series -

Dotty Dishes the Dirt – prequel

Dotty unearths more than she bargains for when she digs up human bones.

Dotty Dices with Death – Book 1

The man of Dotty's dreams turns into a nightmare when he is found dead under suspicious circumstances.

Dotty Dreads a Disaster – Book 2

That's not a pile of old clothes that Dotty discovers lying in the duckpond, it's a body

Dotty Dabbles in Danger – Book 3

Who is the mystery man that was trampled to death by cattle down at Devil's Bridge Farm?

Dotty Discovers Diamonds – Book 4

The lavish birthday party turns to disaster when a man is found murdered.

Printed in Great Britain
by Amazon